Just Desserts: Flash Fiction

Just Desserts: Flash Fiction

MIRIAM N. KOTZIN

Just Desserts

Copyright © 2010

by Miriam N. Kotzin

Cover art and design: Peter Groesbeck

Published by

~Star Cloud Press®~
6137 East Mescal Street
Scottsdale, Arizona 85254-5418

ISBN: 978-1-932842-42-5 — $ 14.95

Library of Congress Control Number: 2010923702

Printed in the United States of America

Table of Contents

Dedicated to
Paul D. Green

Sunshine

CARELESS SUNSHINE splashed onto the floor of the nursery. Emily stood in the doorway, amazed at the bright flood pouring through the window this morning. The golden light glazed the painted wooden furniture. The mobile, stirred by a faint current of air, turned over the crib.

On the bureau the music-box carousel sat where she had left it last week, its horses ready to circle at the turn of a key. Music would play, and the spotted horses would ride up and down on their striped poles.

Sunlight struck the faceted crystal bowl that Emily had set on the changing table, scattering rainbows that clung to the walls and ceiling. The roses in the bowl were pink and yellow, Peace roses they called them.

The tiny flowers in Emily's soft cotton dress were pink and yellow, too. The pillows on the rocker were pink, and the pad on the changing table, and the roses Emily had stenciled on the wall in the months before Lena was born. And before it had been stripped, the crib had been made up with white sheets with pink flowers that were almost the same color as Lena's rosebud mouth.

Emily felt her husband's hand on her shoulder, gentle, tentative. Richard stood with her awhile, looking into the empty room. He wore the same dark blue suit he'd worn when they married. "Emily," he said, "It's time."

Lucky

MOTHER'S DAY, and she's one of the ash blondes on the bus to the casino, clutching her coupon for the buffet and her roll of give-back quarters. Atlantic City's not Vegas, and it's not what it was fifty years ago. Neither is she, but they both look good enough in the right light. So here she is in her red linen suit with a pink shell, wearing red sandals, headed down the shore. Besides her straw handbag, Joan carries a plastic bag from Shop Rite.

When she gets into the casino, she makes her way straight to the ladies room and sets the bags down on the granite counter. She takes out a clear plastic box and opens it as though it held something fragile and precious. Inside, a Cattleya orchid, the purple kind that gives the color "orchid" its name, sits in a white nest of what could pass for leftover Easter grass. The corsage has a stiff bow, shiny pink ribbon.

Joan pins the corsage to her suit jacket. The pink pearl teardrop on the end of the pin peeks out from under the ribbon.

"What a lovely corsage!" says the woman standing next to her. She has pink roses pinned to her white blouse.

"Yours is lovely, too."

"Yes, it is," the woman says, touching her corsage. "It's from my daughter and her husband. We're so lucky." She nods at Joan when she says this.

"That we are," Joan says, preening at the image in the mirror. She opens her purse and takes out a pink lipstick, and runs it over her lips. She sucks her lips between her teeth and rubs them together. "Very lucky, indeed." She bares her teeth and leans forward to check. She never has lipstick on her teeth.

"I guess we'll find out how lucky we are when we get to the slots. My cousin won $250 last week," the woman says. She hesitates and looks in the mirror, touches the roses again. "Well, maybe I don't need to win at the machines. I ought to be grateful for the good luck I have with my son-in-law."

"I know just what you mean," Joan answers. "You can never tell who they'll bring home, can you?"

"Not these days. This is my daughter's second marriage. I have three grandchildren. And you?"

"None yet," says Joan. "I don't believe in pushing. You can't push that way. When a woman's ready to have children she will."

The woman laughs. "When we were young we were expected to get married and have kids right on schedule."

Joan nods.

The woman goes on, "And it was the odd duck who didn't marry! And our parents! How many times did they ask about when we were going to make them grandparents. Today, who knows? Some of these girls will end up alone. We're so lucky."

Joan looks at her watch, smiles at the other woman in the mirror. Yesterday she had gone to ShopRite, and the refrigerator case with flowers caught her eye. "Special," the sign said. "Orchid Corsages for Mother's Day $10!" The case was filled with clear plastic boxes, each with an orchid, some white, some purple, each cradled in a nest of grass, the white in purple grass; the purple, in white.

Joan had taken one of each, had stood for a long time staring into the boxes as though they were crystal balls. She had always hated making choices. "Yes," she answers. "We are lucky, very lucky indeed."

She puts the empty box in the plastic bag and drops them in the trash, then heads out to the smoky floor where lights flash and bells ring from across the room. She takes the roll of quarters from her purse and holds it in her hand. Maybe she'll watch some blackjack or find a craps table where she can stand among the crowd. The dealers and croupiers manage their tables well, and the players are as good a show as any on TV. It doesn't matter, really, where she goes first. She's in no rush. The bus won't leave for hours, and, after all, even then, she will have the whole day to herself.

Civil Ceremonies

THE FOUR OF US were riding in their dad's car when Donny, who was fourteen, said he was afraid of babies. His brother Benny, who was eight, had just volunteered that he was afraid of clowns. I looked around. No clowns or babies within sight.

"What's up, Benny?" I asked, turning around to look at them. The vanity mirror wouldn't do for this.

"Nothin'," he answered. Benny still sucked his thumb, and stopped just long enough to give his answer.

"There won't be any clowns around today, Benny," I said. I hoped I sounded reassuring.

"Ummhumm." He stuck his nose against the car window, an awkward position with his thumb still in his mouth. He was done with me for a while.

"Donny, I didn't know you don't like babies," I said. Their dad wasn't saying anything.

Donny glared. "Don, OK? Don," he paused. "'Donny' was when I was Benny's age," he said, smacking his brother on the arm. Benny didn't pay any attention, didn't even try to swat his brother away.

"I'm sorry, Don. I'll try to remember." I didn't say anything about his hitting his brother.

"Whatever," he said in the typical fuck-you tone used for "whatever."

Before I could turn around he added, "And I didn't say I don't like babies."

"Oh?" I said, my voice brightening.

"No. I said I was afraid of them." His voice had a tone of finality. And then he added, "Like Benny here's afraid of clowns."

Again, when he said "Benny," he smacked him on the arm, this time hard enough for Benny to whine, "Cut it oooout, Donny." He kept his thumb at the ready, so that from a distance it looked as though he were giving the thumbs-up sign.

I admired Benny's mastery of rhetoric. Protest and put-down in four words.

"He's hitting me, Dad," Benny said.

"Tell him you don't like it," his father said. Now I was keeping quiet.

"He knows I don't like it," Benny said. "He's not stupid. He's just mean." He slipped his thumb back into his mouth.

"Well, then, don't pay any attention to him, and he'll stop," his father said.

Donny smacked Benny again, this time hard enough so that I could hear the slap of his open hand on Benny's arm. The suit coat must be of some use in keeping it from hurting, I hoped.

"He's not stopping, Dad." Several more whacks followed this statement.

"Cut it out, Don," his father said.

"He can hit me if he wants to," Donny said. He held out his arm to his brother. His suit jacket was on the floor of the car under his feet.

"Here, hit me. Hit me as hard as you want," Donny said. Benny wasn't having any of it. He kept his thumb in his mouth and his forehead on the window.

"You can punch me in the stomach," Donny said. "Go on."

Benny turned towards Donny, took his thumb out of his mouth and said, "Just because you're an asshole doesn't mean that I have to be one too." He put his thumb back in his mouth.

6

Donny threw his arms around his brother and gave him a bear hug. "I love you, Benny."

"Get off of me," Benny shrieked. The word "me" soared into the higher registers, and he followed it with a plain screech. He does this whenever he's really irritated, which is several times a day. The military should tape that sound and use it as a non-lethal weapon. I want to slap a testosterone patch on him so that his voice will change early.

"See, I hugged him," Donny said. "I'll hug you again, Benny," he said, lunging towards him as far as the seat belt allowed.

Another shriek from Benny. This one is all-star. I put my hand on their dad's thigh, tap it a couple of times.

"Ben. Don," he said. "Both of you. Today isn't the day."

They were quiet a moment, and I asked, careful not to call him "Donny," "Don, why are you afraid of babies?"

"Well, they just lie there and stare at you with those big eyes, you know." He looked up as if the answer were on the car dome-light. "Kinda like aliens. Only helpless."

I folded my hands over my belly. I hadn't started to show. I didn't say what I was thinking, that he must be feeling pretty helpless himself these days.

Benny nodded and said, "Clowns aren't helpless. Babies are."

"That can be scary," I said, thinking of myself and their dad, too.

A Virtually True Account of How Wallace Stevens Wrote "Thirteen Ways of Looking at a Blackbird"

STEVENS SAT AT HIS DESK AT HARTFORD ACCIDENT AND INDEMNITY, leaned back in his worn leather chair and rocked, listening to the comfortable, familiar sound of ancient springs bearing his considerable weight. He sighed. He did not know which he preferred, the sound of the springs or the silence that followed. He jotted a note on his yellow legal pad: "I do not know which to prefer," he wrote, "the springs creaking or just after." That's the ticket, he thought, a sly reference to Keats' "Grecian Urn," his unheard music. Those Harvard years, well, even without the degree, he'd got something. But "springs creaking"? He'd leave it at that for now.

He swivelled towards the window. It was snowing, and, worse, from the looks of it, it was going to snow. He leaned back, folded his hands on his paunch and closed his eyes, conjuring a landscape. What landscape? Key West? Palm trees, sun glinting on cerulean seas? A rivulet of sweat stings his eye. Not Key West, then, today. No, today it must be snowing. A snowy landscape. A mountain, perhaps? Yes. A mountain. A snowy mountain.

He leaned forward and wrote it down. "One snowy mountain." He would stay at his club for dinner instead of dealing with Elsie, who was always irritating, incessantly interrupting him when he was writing. Settled. He'd stay in town. Now content, expansive, he drew a line through "One" and wrote above it, "Twenty." "Twenty mountains?" Then, "A range of snowy mountains." Not idiomatic. Folly to count

8

mountains, though. He imagined a solitary self, counting mountains like sheep on a sleepless night. White sheep. White mountains. "The hills skip like lambs, the mountains like rams." That line's taken, but he was pleased to have thought of it, made counting mountains more plausible, though why must poetry be plausible? These documents on the desk, they're another thing altogether. He'll get to them soon enough.

If mountains, then trees dark against the snow. If trees, then birds. What birds? He closed his eyes: a cardinal perched on a pine limb, and, while Stevens watched, silver letters materialized, sparkled, "Christmas Greetings." Ach! He changed pine to cedar. Even so, the cardinal was impossible. What then? Chickadee? Ridiculous. Tufted titmouse? Worse. He wanted a plain bird. No nonsense. Blackbird. Perfect. That's it, then. He scratched out "springs" and wrote "blackbird."

Then he listened. His own breath—in and out—reminded him of the bellows he used at the dying flame of his hearth, a bit of a wheeze lately, his own tuneless whistle. Right! Whistle. "Blackbird whistling." He wrote, "I do not know which to prefer ....the blackbird whistling or just after." Incomplete, that. What would Keats have written? Surely that master of inflection and innuendo would have written something about beauty.

He turned to the stack of legal documents: "Haddam vs. The Hartford." "Nothing but trouble," he muttered, "the whole scrawny pack of them." The poem would have to wait.

Cindy's Case

THE WOMAN from Child Protection Services, who had just been assigned this case, noted that the house was clean, almost abnormally so. Perhaps they had spiffed up to ready for her visit. She checked her records. Cindy was seventeen, almost eighteen, and ready to go out on her own.

The sofa and all the chairs had fluffy throw pillows with elaborate embroidery and needlepoint floral designs. She picked one up and examined it more closely. "Lovely," she murmured.

"Oh! Do you really like them?" Cindy asked, "I do them for fun in my spare time after I finish my homework and chores." Her blue eyes sparkled with joy at the compliment.

Children ought to have household responsibilities, thought the woman from CPS, and this room looks homey, its hearth swept clean. "You and the other girls help out around the house. That's nice…"

"No, ma'am, Lucy and Clara don't do housework. It's not good for them." Cindy shook her head, her short blonde ponytail bouncing.

"I'm sorry they're ill," she said.

"It's just that they have real sensitive skin. They'd break their nails if they did the cleaning, and scrubbing the pots would ruin their manicures and make their skin yucky. They'd wear gloves, but they have a latex allergy that makes them break out something awful."

"Oh?"

"They do their homework, but they're frail, and have to rest a lot. They're not strong like me. Scrubbing pots doesn't hurt my nails. See?" Cindy extended her hands to the woman from CPS. Her hands were strong, but feminine, with beautifully shaped oval nails.

"I've met your stepfather. He said the girls were decorating the gym. He said I could wait here for you. He seemed in a big hurry to leave."

"Probably. He had to pick up some last-minute things for the after-prom party we're having tonight. And I'll have a lot to do when he gets back—flower arranging, decorating, making cookies and sandwiches. I'm making omelets too," Cindy said, with pride.

The woman thought she heard a wistful note beneath the pride in accomplishment. "How are you going to do all that and go to the prom?" she asked.

For the first time, a shadow passed across Cindy's face. "I'm not going. I don't have a dress or shoes. I don't have a job, and my allowance, well, it goes for my regular clothes," she said, with a gesture at her Walmart jeans and no-name sneakers.

"You didn't want an after-school job?"

"I would have liked one, or baby-sitting. But I don't really have time, not with my homework and cooking dinner for the family and keeping up with chores. You know, laundry, cleaning—not just dusting but doing the floors and windows. The floors get much cleaner when you get on your hands and knees. I like things to sparkle. And there are yard things to keep up with. I really like to garden, and I grow almost all of our vegetables. I can things for the winter. Fruit, too."

Dear me, poor thing, the woman from CPS thought. She opened Cindy's folder and skimmed through the previous visits. Then she paged through and found a longer observation, which she read: "Cindy Ella is a seventeen-year-old Caucasian female, with a pleasant demeanor and a neat and clean appearance. She dresses modestly. Cindy does well enough in school, carrying a B+ average in the business track. She expresses no desire to go to college or pursue any education past high school.

"Her extensive personality tests show that she suffers from several psychological disorders, including mild agoraphobia, and is unwilling to venture far from the home.

"Her tests also indicate an Obsessive Compulsive Disorder, which seems to be worsening and ought to be watched, with possible future assignment to a psychiatrist for evaluation as a candidate for therapy and use of psychotropic medication such as Prozac, which has proved useful in such cases. The OCD manifests in the client's preoccupation with housework and in an apparent inability to tolerate anything less than perfection, both in orderliness of her surroundings and what she calls, "wanting things to sparkle."

"Furthermore, she seems to exhibit traits of social anxiety, and appears to have no desire to have friends outside the family, to participate in after-school activities, or to have a job. For example, she refuses to attend any of the school dances and, instead, invents excuses of having to stay home to prepare party food, although she will not participate in the party, except to serve the food. Being behind a table or holding a tray seems to alleviate her anxiety as it relieves her from the responsibility of significant interaction with her peers. Perhaps Paxil would relieve her social anxiety. However, it is not clear whether the social anxiety is real, or a by-product of her OCD and consequent preoccupation with housework, or whether it is another manifestation of agoraphobia.

"Her home placement is appropriate. She is in a close-knit family, with two other girls near to her in age. The family seems to tolerate her aberrations and they have accommodated to her pathology. They allow her to exercise self-determination in her household activities, putting up with her almost continual pillow fluffing, floor scrubbing, and other cleaning activities. The family eats whatever she cooks although Cindy's talents do not appear to be culinary in nature.

"Cindy Ella is a troubled young woman, whose demeanor is disarming. The careless caseworker might easily misinterpret Cindy's role in the household and wrongly see her as a victim. Cindy unconsciously encourages such a view."

The woman from CPS looked at Cindy again. Strange, she thought, she seemed so normal at first. I almost felt sorry for her. Shows how first impressions can be so wrong. I'm sure I'll get better at this when I have more experience, she thought. And I've got to read the whole case folder before I make my home visits.

Freudian Slip

I WAS in the lingerie section, fingering the goods. I plunged my hands into a pile of panties. A sales woman in a chocolate cashmere sweater stared. She kept her eyes on my face while I opened and closed my fists over and over again.

"May I help you?" she said.

I kept my hands down in the pile, but I thought to compose myself enough to smile at her. Pause, I said to myself, collect yourself, but oh, the silk, the silk, the silk... and then I said, "No thanks. I'm just lurking."

Two of a Kind

. . − . . . −

AGNES LEANED on the horn. She caught the eyes of the driver in the car ahead of her as he looked into his rear-view mirror.

He raised his hand, flipping her the bird.

She tapped out F U in Morse code on the horn, the only useful skill remaining from all her years teaching civil defense in the fifties.

Young people today have no respect for the elderly.

. . − . . − − −

Eric slammed on his breaks. The woman behind him leaned on her horn.

It's a red light, lady.

He looked into his rear-view mirror and exchanged glares with a Blue-Hair, barely able to see over her wheel.

Eric flipped the bird.

Damned if she didn't honk, spelling F U. Where'd she learn Morse Code?

He beeped U 2, glad he remembered something from his years as an Eagle Scout.

Souvenir

THE MORNING after he returned, Lissy discovered treasure on the hall table, beach glass: cobalt, sea green, ice blue, amber, moonstone. She held the shards in her palm, lifted them up to her face. She hoped she might find a whiff of distant sea. Instead she found a sickly sweet smell she didn't recognize.

She carried the glass into the bedroom where David was adjusting his tie. She stood watching as he held his head back, and tugged the knot up to his collar. He looked like a kid when he did that, she thought, concentrating so hard, the tip of his tongue protruding.

"I found these," she said, holding out her hand. "So pretty!"

"Yeah," he said, glancing at what she held, then turning back to the mirror, "it took me hours."

Clutching the sea glass in one fist, she put her arms around his waist and gave him a hug. So romantic, she thought, to think of me every time he walked on the beach.

She pictured the Pacific in winter, waves pounding the shore, the rush of the water, the sand under bare feet.

"There was lots of seaweed, with big bladders you could pop. Tons of it. But I couldn't find any shells." He pulled the tie's knot undone, readjusted the ends, and started over. He cursed under his breath. "Somebody said there are, like, whole forests of this big seaweed, kelp, actually."

"The beach glass is beautiful," she said. "I love it." Double Windsor, she thought, Half-Windsor, Four-in-hand. She'd learned to tie all these knots in her twenties. She could stand in front of him and do the tie perfectly. She used to.

16

"It is pretty, isn't it?"

She heard the satisfaction in his voice. "Like old jewels, David," she said, "Thank you!"

"It's not for you," he said. "Tanya asked me to bring her shells and beach glass."

His secretary had asked him to bring her shells and beach glass? I wish I'd asked, Lissy thought. "It's all for her? I can't keep any of it?" As soon as she'd spoken, she was sorry.

"It's for Tanya," he said. His voice was tight. Was he annoyed at her or the tie he couldn't get right? The wrong end was still too long. "She asked for it," he repeated.

Lissy smelled the glass again, wondering if that was a perfume, or just hotel soap. "I wanted to go with you," she said, even though he knew that.

"If you had wanted me to bring you something you could have asked."

"I could have," She paused. "I wanted to be with you."

"Yeah," he said, "but you weren't, were you." He leaned forward and tugged at the patterned silk. "Look, I called you didn't I?"

"Every day," she said, remembering hurried phone calls, stilted conversation. He'd always seemed to be headed out to the beach or just getting back. She watched him working at his tie. This time he'd got it right. He looked into the mirror and frowned, caught her eye.

It was the angle of incidence, she thought, remembering her physics, and the angle of reflection. They had to be just right for this to happen. She could see him and he could see her. He was talking to her reflection. But she couldn't see her own face in the mirror. "Every day," she repeated.

"If you'd wanted me to bring you something, to get you shells or beach glass or jewelry, you should have asked," he said. "I would have."

He held out his hand for the beach glass. "Look, be reasonable," he said, "there's not much here. And I promised her."

"What would have happened if I had asked too?" Lissy said. "What would you have done then? Would I have got first pick?" She stared at his upturned palm.

"Don't be such a baby," he said, "I don't have time for this. Come on, Lissy, give it here." He tapped his palm.

Would he pry her fingers open? Or grab her wrist and twist until she opened her fist and all the glass lay scattered on the floor? Would he tell her to pick it up, or squat and get it himself?

Lissy dropped the glass into David's hand. *Kleinekeiten*, she told herself, they were fighting over something worthless, almost nothing. She looked at the colored glass for a moment before his fingers closed over it and he dropped it into his pants pocket.

She'd clutched the shards so tightly they had dug into her palm, and she could still feel some sensation. It was so real that when the door had closed she looked at her hand, almost amazed to find it empty.

Pesto

ALL ALONG THE STREET these first cold nights have set the trees to simmering with gaudy autumn fires. Where the sun stays longest on the trees, the green maples are tipped with gold and orange. The ginkgos with their yellow fan-like leaves are stinking torches along the driveway.

Before it's too late I'll harvest all the basil and the last of the tomatoes in the garden. I'll make pesto with the basil and freeze what we don't use tonight. I've gone to the cheese shop in the mall for Parmigiano-Reggiano and Romano. And I've stopped on the way home for good walnuts and a baguette at Trader Joe's. I got an early start, so I'm in no rush.

I wrap the unripe tomatoes in newspaper, put them in a paper bag in the cellar and pin a note about them on the corkboard. I put the ripe tomatoes, red and gold like the leaves, in a wooden bowl on the kitchen table.

In his blue and black costume and whiteface, Picasso's Harlequin stares, but not at me. Unwatched, I grate the cheese into a bowl. I strip the basil leaves from their stems. I toss the basil leaves, garlic cloves, a handful of parsley and the walnuts into the food processor. I drizzle in the dark-green virgin olive oil while the food processor whirls. As I watch, in moments, the whole leaves are reduced to a pulp. I stir this mixture with the cheeses in the bowl, add just a pinch or two of salt, a little ground pepper, and my secret, a few scrapes of nutmeg. Today making pesto seems like an act of violence.

I set the table for our dinner, napkin and forks to the left of the plate, knife and spoon to the right. I make sure that the patterns on the plates face in the same direction at both place settings. I put the last of

19

the roses from the garden in a small vase in the center of the table, tea lights on either side in little glass bowls.

I find the bottle of Cabernet that we saved so long for a special occasion. I cut the foil and remove the cork. The cork is whole, sound, a good sign. I set the wine on the table, letting it breathe.

I take a deep breath myself. And then another. Tomorrow I will leave. Tonight dinner will be perfect. Later, as, separate, we tell our stories, each of us will take credit for being, *comme on dit*, so fucking civilized.

The Answer

THE NEXT WEEK I returned and found your house filled with the smell of rotting fruit. "David?" A tiny storm of fruit flies rose, frantic, scattering. The peaches had darkened to sepia and raw umber, furred blue and gray. "Duddy, are you here?"

Crumpled gold paper and white silk ribbon lay on the table next to the celadon bowl. "It's me."

The heavy brass candlesticks stood empty.

I picked up the stiff paper and folded it into a neat square. I rolled the ribbon around my fingers and set it next to the paper. "Are you here?" Nothing in your house answered.

That night I had closed the black velvet box, and with the muffled snap, I thought it would be all over, as the swift fall of the curtain signals the certain end of a tragic opera. But you said, "No," an echo refusing my refusal, and so we sat, each of us stunned, separate, watching the candles gutter. The flickering, failing light, merciless, flung our shadows on opposite walls.

Ramona

SOMETIMES MY HUSBAND talks in his sleep. Last night he said, "Ramona." I wish I hadn't heard him.

When he's awake and he talks about Ramona, Jim's face gets the same glow as it gets, even now after all these years, when he holds me in his arms.

We first met Ramona at a party when she was an au pair for a couple we knew only slightly. Strawberry blonde, ringlets around her pale face, she'd glided through their living room with the younger of their children in her arms. That night when we came home, Jim said that he would be surprised if Ramona were an effective au pair because she was such a china doll. At the time it didn't seem like a compliment. When the couple moved away, we heard nothing more of Ramona.

And then, nearly a decade later, she answered an ad we'd placed on the bulletin board of the organic coop. But, as Jim said when she came to work for us, she'd become a different woman. "Woman," he said, not "china doll." Her curly hair had been cut short, and she was even sleeker than she'd been when we had first seen her.

Ramona had finished her stint as an au pair, had married brilliantly, and then, less brilliantly, divorced, being left with domicile, dog, and debt. Baby-sitting, she said, supplemented the income she had from her job in the bakery. She'd never finished college, believing her husband would support her. The marriage had been recent enough that she still wore fine clothes, gold bangle bracelets and rings on both hands.

"I never wear hoop earrings when I baby sit," she'd said. "Kids like to grab them and pull. I learned that soon enough."

22

"Ours are old enough not to do that," I'd said. The next time she came, though she didn't wear hoops, she wore chandelier earrings so long that they brushed her neck. I was sorry I'd said anything. The kids didn't pull them. Jimmy climbed right onto her lap and poked at the earring with his chubby index finger so the earring swung back and forth glittering in the lamplight.

Last Thursday Jim came home from his poker game, and I heard the tone in his voice that I had come to associate with Ramona. For a moment I thought I'd been wrong. He was talking like that, glowing, when he hadn't been anywhere near her. But before that thought could settle itself and swell into joy, Jim kept on talking, and it turned out that the subject of the evening's conversation had been Ramona, Ramona, Ramona. Wall-to-wall Ramona. The perils of Ramona. Ramona tied to railroad tracks by a mustachioed villain. Ramona ready for rescue. Each of the men had a story about the ill-used Ramona and her valor, and apparently Jim never once thought how odd that was.

Later that night, he looked at me with the lit-up face I'd once thought of as belonging only to me, but which now I thought of as hers, too. "You know what I'm thinking," he said, a little private ritual we'd developed.

I answered on cue, "You love me." Usually this response would be followed by at least one kiss, often more. Not then.

"Do you know what you said?"

I nodded, and he went on, "You said, 'You love me,' You emphasized me."

I told myself that he'd never have dared say that if he had the smallest idea of his feelings about Ramona. I vowed I wasn't going to be the one to tell him.

At dinner we'd been talking about what had happened during the day. I was saying how I'd spoken to one of my students and urged her to go to college, to make sure she could earn a good living. I'd told her that even if you married a successful man, you could never tell what might happen and that you might need to support yourself and maybe children. "I was thinking of Ramona," I said. Though Ramona had no children. Yet.

Jim was indignant. "My Ramona?" he said. "You think that begins to describe what happened to her."

"How many Ramonas are there?" I murmured, not even saying what I wanted to scream, "What makes her your Ramona?"

I looked at our children, Jimmy drawing patterns in his mashed potatoes with his fork. Ellen, almost nine, sitting wide-eyed.

"Only one Ramona," Jimmy said. Ellen nodded, solemn.

"Yes," I said, keeping my tone as flat as I could.

Smoke

HE WAS SORRY he had given up smoking. He hadn't stopped smoking yet, but he'd told everyone that he was going to stop, and that was almost as bad. Lighting up now was considered a visible act of moral failure, of weakness so profound that had he been another sort of fellow he would have felt guilty.

He wanted a cigarette even though it was too late in the day to get the satisfying click in the lungs. He wanted the comfort of habitual actions to carry him through this conversation. He fumbled in his jacket pocket until his fingers met the smooth metal of the gold monogrammed cigarette case she had bought for him. She'd told him she had discovered it in an antique store and presented it to him like found treasure. The initials in the monogram, of course, were not his.

"I thought you'd given up smoking," she said, with a nod at the case. She turned in her seat to signal to the waiter who was hovering over a nearby table.

"I said I was thinking about giving up smoking." A flame danced at the tip of his cigarette. In a moment he would inhale and drop the dead match in the ashtray of this restaurant that he had chosen because it still allowed smoking. He looked at the cigarette, its smoke scrawling upwards in curls and dashes that he imagined were marvelous revelations written in a language he had failed to learn as a child.

She raised a single eyebrow and shifted in her seat. The waiter had disappeared into the kitchen. She sat watching for his reappearance.

"Another late night, darling?" He stubbed out the cigarette, and snapped open the case to light a second.

"But the project should be finished soon."

He watched as her single dimple appeared on her left cheek.

"And then we can do anything we want."

Before he lit the cigarette, he tapped it on the table, an old habit. "This weekend...?" He inhaled deeply, knocked the ash off into the ashtray.

"Nothing would please me more," she said. Her words and her tone were honey. Only someone who knew her well would recognize the tell, the dimple she had when she lied.

He knew her well. Moreover, she'd told him about the dimple herself, when their relationship was fresh, and a lie unimaginable. For months he's been seeing the dimple; for months he's kept silent, preferring to watch and learn. After all, he had nothing to lose.

The Patsy

SHE CUPS her hands over the candle. "You're such a cynic." The better part of her fillet sits cold.

I could counter by asking her why she is such a patsy, but if I keep quiet, she will glide through her litany of complaints, and we'll have a pleasant evening.

Her otherwise bare arms are braceleted with gold and amethyst, four bangles, one for each year. She rarely wears them, complaining that they snag her sweaters. I've tucked a fifth, gift-wrapped, into my jacket pocket.

She'll hold her arm out to me, and I'll slip the bracelet over her small hand. The clasp will make a satisfying click as I fasten it on her arm with the others.

"Mr. Stone Face." She cuts a dainty piece of meat, but does not fork it into her perfect mouth. On her plate, ovals of fat congeal on the surface of a red pool.

Her lips open and close. From time to time through her white teeth I glimpse her tongue. Her words float above her head like a Lichtenstein print. Her eyelashes curl long and thick. Her blonde hair shines in the candlelight. A fat tear on her cheek would complete the illusion.

I place my hands, palms down, on the wooden table and watch the bubble of words float, harmless, to the ceiling.

Just Desserts

DAVIS STROKED his tie. Lorraine recognized the gesture of self-satisfaction. This was different from the knot-adjusting gesture, which she translated as a personal battening of the hatches.

"Of course," Lorraine said. She set her fork and knife on her plate, fork tines down, knife next to the fork, both pointing to the center of the plate. Much of her food remained. She looked at it with some regret. She'd found the chipotle glazed salmon tasty, the mashed garlic-infused potatoes delightful, the crisp, sauteed snow peas exceptionally sweet.

Davis continued eating his prime rib. For a man of his age he was an intrepid diner. "You'd be quite an attractive woman, really," he said. "I've been wanting to tell you for a while." His thick prime rib sat in a lake of pink juice. Lorraine did not eat red meat.

He smiled. The candle in the center of the table flickered in an otherwise imperceptible current of air. A stem of Phalaenopsis orchid and a few strands of bear grass trembled in a bud vase.

In the ladies room Lorraine peered at her reflection in the mirror. Davis could be a wonderful conversationalist; too bad he'd turned to this topic. She leaned forward to examine her face, frowning. She checked her figure, turning right and left. She poked her finger into her ribs; her flesh was soft, she thought, not flabby. If the waiter hadn't removed her plate, she might have just one more bite or so of that salmon.

Davis himself had gone slack in the manner of aging athletes. Lorraine closed her eyes and thought about his long body lying next to hers, how she'd wakened, and noticed his loosening skin. Flaccid was the word that came to her mind when she thought of him.

So she understood his desire for a lithe woman, one on whom gravity's pull was not so evident. She squeezed her upper arm. Soft. She sighed, thinking of dessert. It's a pity, she thought, that crème caramel was out of fashion. She thought about a mound of flan, sitting in a pool of dark syrup, with a hint of bitterness to set off the sweet.

Davis ordered coffee and crème brulée. Lorraine considered the delight of breaking through the crisp sugar crust and sinking her spoon into the custard, the contrast in her mouth between the crunch of the sugar and the cream. Davis looked at her meaningfully. She knew she was expected to order the mixed berries, a crystal dish filled with perfect looking strawberries and raspberries. But the berries were out of season, and though beautiful to the eye were bound to be nearly flavorless. "Just coffee," she said. Davis rewarded her with a smile and another stroke of his tie. The waiter was just turning away, when she added, "No, please. I'll have the crème brulée as well."

She smiled at Davis, said in her softest voice, "Life has so few pleasures these days." She watched him flush. She took a sip of her water. The waiter had refilled her glass while she was gone. The ice shimmered in the candlelight. "I know you understand, darling." She put an ever-so-slight emphasis on "you."

She placed her hand on the table to see if he would take it. Instead he refolded his napkin, and checked his watch. He understood perfectly. Had she been wearing a tie, she would have run her fingers down its entire length. She savored the feeling. They were sharing, after all, their just desserts.

Perfectly Sober

SHELDON LOOKED AROUND the room. People were talking in groups, their shoulders so tight together that if they'd been bent down they could've been in football huddles. But then they wouldn't have been able to hold their plates of brie and crackers or their drinks. He smiled at his thought and checked his watch. Only a few minutes left.

He and Marcia were thought to be so civilized, these days attending the same parties. He did not want to be the one to break the illusion. And he was afraid that if he said no, he'd never be invited again. He wasn't ready for the division of the friends; they'd already divided the books, the silver, and the china. The children were old enough to bounce back and forth during their college vacations as it suited them. They were with him tonight, but both out at their own parties.

The TV was on, of course, as it had been all evening without sound; until now it had been no more important than the wallpaper. He turned up the volume. The crowd in Times Square was allowed its voice. Sheldon heard a lurid description of the heightened security measures protecting them all. Then the focus was on the clock and the ball atop the tower. He and Marcia had watched this American ritual together for twenty-seven years.

The countdown was about to start, and all the groups opened to face the screen. His host and hostess walked into the room carrying trays of little plastic cups, champagne or Perrier. He took Perrier and smiled his thanks.

Ten...nine...eight...seven...

He stayed off to one side to watch. Across the room Marcia was wearing a new black dress and the rope of pearls he'd given her on her fiftieth birthday.

Six…five…four…. She held a plastic glass of champagne. She hadn't stopped when he had. A pity, he thought. He allowed himself the illusion that they might have stayed together.

Three….two….one….and then "Happy New Year." A flurry of hugs and round-robin kisses. Air kisses, phony European-style kisses, and Marcia's back toward him through all the kissing.

The hostess turned off the TV and with her husband started singing "Auld Lang Syne," and Sheldon joined in. Their group had been doing this for years, and, for years, going home in their car, Marcia had mocked the custom. Tonight her soprano was as loud as though she'd been asked to lead the singing. He heard his voice crack, and he stopped singing. He did not even mouth the words. Marcia raised her empty glass, as if in a toast to him, and kept on singing.

They had laughed about the lyrics, puzzled, what should be forgotten and never brought to mind. By the end they'd given up on finding the answer. It was too late now, but he knew he'd think about it again tonight, alone on the drive home, taking it slow, mindful of those drunk drivers, their laughter and arguments filling their cars until there was room for nothing more, except the promise of a night cap.

Sheldon raised his glass to Marcia. He'd never much liked Perrier. He drained the glass anyhow.

Tines

EVEN BY CANDLELIGHT she could see he was bored. She noticed something wrong about his mouth when he wasn't eating or talking, not a tic, exactly, but a recurring expression of impatience.

"Finished?" he asked.

Caesar salad covered half her plate. Cara sighed.

"Something wrong?" he asked.

"Do you think they use raw eggs in this dressing?"

"No one does that any more." He paused and said, "Why did you order it?"

He'd ordered for her. Nobody does that anymore either. She hadn't protested. He'd asked her to dinner, and he'd be paying. If he wanted to get her Caesar salad, Caesar salad it would be. She shrugged, "It seemed right at the time."

"This was a mistake," he said. His fork lay, tines down, in the center of his plate. He'd had enough.

She had, too. She'd eat the salad, though.

"This is where my wife told me she wanted a divorce. Ex-wife. Almost."

"Why?"

"She said I was..."

"I meant, then why come here?" She took a sip of water, ate a bite of salad. What would he have said if she hadn't interrupted him? Anyway, men never told the truth about their wives. How could they?

"Not afraid of food poisoning any more?"

"Not afraid of anything." She chose a pale piece of Romaine. Anchovies. This was the real-deal dressing.

"She was."

Cara tore off a small piece of her roll. She eyed the butter in the ceramic crock. It would be soft enough to spread without making a mess. Salt or sweet? She made a bet with herself. Sweet.

"She had blue eyes."

"What?"

"She was what she was. She had blue eyes. She was afraid."

"They're not the same thing," she said. She had nothing to lose by disagreeing. The butter was colder than she'd thought. She put a curl of it on her plate, then spread a small amount on her roll.

"Look at me, will you?" he said.

She had been paying rather a lot of attention to her food, hadn't she? It promised to be the best of the dinner.

"Brown," he said. "You have brown eyes."

"I know."

"I don't know why I hadn't noticed. I usually do."

Usually? She ate the morsel of roll. The butter was sweet. "It doesn't matter, does it? My eye-color?"

"No," he said, "I guess it doesn't."

What color were his eyes? From this distance she couldn't tell. And it didn't matter, did it? She was finished, after all. She sighed and placed her fork on her plate, tines down.

Brood

THE BRAZEN DOME of the cicadas' high-pitched drone claps down tight. All day I have been trapped in relentless sound.

Cicadas cling to every shrub and tree, long lacy wings and big orange eyes. They fly, hover, mate, and start the seventeen-year cycle again. This is the summer of Brood X.

I pull the windows shut, but their sound seeps into the house like a well-deserved reproach. I never thought it would be like this.

A few weeks from now, they will be gone. This time I will outstay them. A dust devil skims across the drive. I watch the sky turn green. We can use a good rain.

Someday, I will recall these details to tell the story of the summer of our divorce. I will begin with a brazen dome.

Undertow

WALKING HERE in the late afternoon, my feet sank ankle deep in sun-warmed sand. I lie on the thin blanket we used on our bed when we were first married. Beneath me the sand is firm as a mattress. If I were to reach out over the edge of the blanket, I could let it trickle, my hand an hourglass.

Once you gathered shells and arranged them on my back in a mosaic. I lay still until you were satisfied with what you had done. The photo is in the album I keep on the top shelf of the closet. What did you take with you when you left?

I lie face up, listening to the waves breaking. I imagine them rise, sparkling droplets of spray caught and blown back by the wind while the green body of the wave curls and crashes and rushes towards the beach, slows as it reaches the end of its journey, leaves a white spindrift record of itself, then retreats. I count silently, timing the waves, and my breathing slows until I stop counting.

I keep my eyes shut, and the whole world is a scarlet glow.

Easy

I LIE with my hands folded, fingers interlaced, like a grade-school student in prayer, like someone lying locked in eternal silence. I listen to his breathing, even and slow. I try to match mine to his. I can't. Too far apart, like long strides, taking him away from me.

At dinner our silence hung like a thick curtain between us until I drew it aside. "What time did you get back from lunch?"

"It was a working lunch."

"You were on voicemail all afternoon."

"Your point is?" He cut so hard his knife scraped the plate.

My point was that he'd said nothing about the meeting he'd been talking about for days and his hair smelled like a shampoo we don't use. "I wanted to meet you in town tonight. I was shopping." Some lies are easy. "When I didn't reach you, I just came on home."

"What did you get?"

"I didn't find it. Something for Ella's daughter and her fiancé." So easy.

I notice that the clock is blinking 12:00, 12:00 12:00. The power must have gone off for a while some time after we'd gone to bed. Funny how you can be without something and not miss it at all, and then see some little sign that it had been gone, but it's back now. Or you just notice it's gone, maybe forever, and when it went missing you don't even know.

Even Without Hills

MOSTLY I KEEP MY HANDS on the wheel at ten and two, though long stretches go by at four and eight. Either way, we stay on this narrow straight road cut through scrub pine. The mountain laurel is just beginning to bloom, and you tell me again how lucky we are to be together now, how perfect the two of us are. Nothing could be better, you say.

Shafts of sunlight fall through the upper stories of the trees to spotlight the mountain laurel. You say you're sorry that we don't have time to pull over on the sandy shoulder of the road to take a closer look. I agree, but I know that even if we had time we wouldn't be stopping.

Every so often we see an unpaved road cut through the woods. Some roads are blocked with an orange metal gate. All are private. I imagine a small cabin, a wood stove, a table with two chairs, fresh coffee, crusty bread and sweet butter with honey, a bright quilt on the bed, an old-fashioned wooden cradle.

"We can come back next week."

I nod. I always liked listening to your promises.

"The mountain laurel will still be in bloom. It will be even better."

"Yes," I answer.

"Really," you say in the tone you use when I disagree with you.

"In a few hours it will be all done with. Next week we won't have so much on our minds."

You tell me again how easy it will be, how simple it is. You use the word, "painless."

In the rear-view mirror I watch the lines slide behind us, one after the other, dash dash dash. I look for the dots, for something, even an SOS, to make sense of the random marks we leave behind.

Casseroles

CASSEROLES — his icebox and its freezer were full of them. More, Abe thought, than he'd eaten in the forty-two years he'd been married to Ida. She hadn't been much for casseroles. She'd dismissed the poverty of thought that resorted to casseroles as a way of using leftovers, had scorned the trend of opening cans of tuna and boiling noodles, adding peas and canned mushroom soup, cans of water chestnuts and bean sprouts. "Again with the canned mushroom soup," she'd say.

"What is this?" she'd said once, flicking her index finger on a recipe for casseroles topped with crumbled potato chips. The newspaper had made a satisfying snap as her finger connected.

All the casseroles were in Corning ware, mostly with a blue and white pattern. The containers had come with written instructions for reheating in oven or microwave. Each had been brought with good wishes, assurances that he needn't rush to return the vessel—and promises of refills.

Chicken and mushroom noodle casserole. Tuna noodle casserole. Beef with red and green pepper casserole. Cheese and potato casserole, low fat cheese, he'd been assured, really quite healthy.

He'd leaned toward Ida to peer at the recipe in the Sunday paper. He didn't see what was the big deal, potato chips, Chinese noodles, or cans of Durkee fried onions. Ida wasn't going to make it. He wasn't going to eat it. A waste of time this fussing. "Well, what do you know," he'd said. He'd leaned over farther and kissed her cheek, then gone back to his own reading.

He bent into the refrigerator, contemplating his choices. Funny, the things you remember, he said aloud, startled by the sound of his voice.

Pawn

SEVERANCE PAY, they called it. The phrase reminded Dina of a hacked body with limbs tossed into random dumpsters. But she took the money, sublet her apartment, and drove out West.

She passed through a series of desert landscapes. She learned that cottonwoods grow along arroyos, and thereafter when she saw the trees, in spite of the arid land she thought "water."

In the late afternoons Dina drove straight into the glare. The visors were useless. She held her hand between her eyes and the sun, and kept on driving as though the setting sun itself were her destination.

The new highways bypassed the small towns, sucking cars past them. When she could, Dina drove on the old roads that were the main street of these towns.

In each town there'd be a shop selling pawn in the back of a grocery, a counter, its case filled with turquoise and silver jewelry, necklaces and bracelets with hammered designs, belt buckles encrusted with nuggets. Dina was drawn to these cases. New jewelry seemed obscenely pristine.

At the end of her third week on the road, she turned off into a town where abandoned pastel cinderblock motels lined the street, their neon signs aching to buzz back to life. The stores had all closed for the day; Dina spotted the pawnshop and promised herself she'd go in the morning.

She'd seen the row of dusty cars parked along the buildings of the Rainbow Motel, which had the expected sign over a glowing "vacancy" notice and a small kidney-shaped swimming pool from the fifties. A woman sat reading in a lounge chair, while two children splashed in the pool.

Dina'd been staying at motels like this, with the only phone stuck on the outside wall of the office and faded green corrugated fiberglass overhangs. Often a swamp cooler filled one corner of the room. Here, she was lucky, it was already on. Some nights she'd waited hours for the room to cool enough to sleep. A blue plastic armchair with duct-tape patches balanced the furniture arrangements. The bed was low, uneven, but she'd been told this was the last room.

She ate her dinner. The last of the grapes and a sandwich.

Tired, she took a quick shower and got into bed. Lucky this motel had a lamp bright enough to read by. She'd learned to carry a 75-watt light bulb with her—that and a roll of toilet tissue.

She got into bed, found the sheets surprisingly cool. She'd been reading a while, when the sheet beneath her felt wet. She checked and found an area about eight inches wide, definitely wet. She pulled the sheet out from the mattress, which was soaked with what she thought was water.

With no way to phone the office, she hauled herself into her clothes. "No Vacancy" shimmered pink under the lit rainbow.

The desk clerk was unperturbed. He said he'd turn the mattress over if she'd give him a hand—there were no spares. With any luck, the water wouldn't have soaked all the way through.

They put the linens on the armchair and together heaved the mattress to its other side. Blood. Unmistakably, blood. It hadn't yet darkened, and the cover of the box spring bore its mark like an abstract print.

They turned the mattress back to the other side. The mattress must have gotten wet when the maid tried to clean off the blood that had seeped through. "Are you sure there aren't any other mattresses anywhere? Maybe a room that has an extra bed that can be switched."

"Just one room like that," he said, "And it's booked." He jerked his head indicating the woman with her children, who were just leaving the pool. "I can phone ahead to the next town, but not likely there'd be a vacancy this late."

She knew he was right. And no use asking him if they should call the police.

The desk attendant gave her a large plastic bag and two thin bath towels as "extra". He sounded bored as though this happened regularly. The maid had left hours ago, and maybe it was just as well. Some questions she didn't care to ask. Dina spread out the plastic bag and, over that, the two towels. She'd sleep on it, she thought, and did.

In the town's pawnshop a man, half her age, stood behind the counter. His straight dark hair hung down his back. Dina could not keep him anchored on the speckled green linoleum floor. He rode a brown horse, held a rifle in the air, his hair streaming behind him.

Dina felt herself blush. She asked to see a squash-blossom necklace, put it on. It hung heavy. She was shrinking.

A large woman in jeans walked in, her black hair tied up in the back with white wool. She put a silver and turquoise bracelet on the counter. "You usually give me one hundred fifty for this."

He nodded.

"Can you do better, today?"

Dina busied herself staring at the jewelry in the case across the room. She imagined women pawning and redeeming until they failed to bring in their payment. Or the day when they arrived with no thought of redemption. These women crowded, surrounded, jostled her until Dina could scarcely catch her breath.

The woman was gone. Dina put the squash-blossom necklace back on the counter. She slipped off her watch and amethyst ring, removed her gold hoop earrings, set them all next to the necklace. Stripped, she asked him, "What can you give me?"

She knew she would take whatever he offered.

Showtime

ART PUSHED HIS EMPTY MUG across the bar. He wiped his mouth with the back of his hand. "TV blew up last week."

Teddy murmured, just as though she hadn't heard this every day since Art had come in stinking of Shalimar and chagrin.

"It happens, Artie, sooner or later," I said. We watched the head rise above the rim. "If you're lucky, later.

"It never runs over," I said, part honest praise, part hope I'd head off Art's story.

It didn't work.

He sprinkled salt on his beer. "Of course, it was just a table model, no loss, not much anyway."

"You ever see Darlene again?" I asked, taking mean-spirited delight in knowing the answer, even as we sat here in splendid fellowship.

"But the insurance won't cover the fire-damage."

I didn't push the Darlene issue.

He stared into the mug like he might find something down in there that he'd want to keep.

Teddy poured me a gin. Warm.

The three of us spent some time talking about insurance, how it never covers what you really want to protect. We're in here, as safe as certified vampires.

We never even got into deductibles.

Over the bar, the television screen flickered, closed captioned. "Can't you turn that off?"

"Sorry, Artie. The boss says ..."

"It's just that this show reminds me. It's what was on that afternoon." His voice rose like the whine of a single-engine plane climbing too steep, too fast.

"This here's her favorite show." He didn't ask Teddy to switch the channel. "She's probably watching it right now,"

I said he was probably right about that.

Then he started on how he'd wanted to have sex, and Darlene had said okay, but only if she could watch Oprah at the same time. He tried, but it didn't work. When he asked for a little help, she divided her attention between the TV and him, mostly paying attention to the TV, though she swore to him that she was doing her best. Now this, I personally doubt, as Darlene could raise the dead in 43 seconds. But I didn't interrupt to venture my opinion, and he went on, "So I grab the lamp, throw it at the television — perfect aim, right through the screen — knock it off the stand, candle topples over into the wastebasket. Smoke detector... firemen busting in."

"Idiot...," I muttered. I stared up at the TV and the credits, like I was really interested in who did the makeup or catering for Oprah. It was about time.

"They're all bitches," he said. Teddy didn't flinch. "Present company excepted."

Barely a minute after the show was over, the bar phone rang. We all could guess who was calling. And I, well, I knew the bell tolled for me.

Cowboy Poet

PROBABLY BECAUSE JAMIE HAD WARNED ME about the cowboy at the end of the bar, told me that he'd call me "Sugar" and I'd melt, I took it as a challenge. I picked up my half-empty Appletini, sidled down to where he sat, and stood between him and the suit to his right.

They weren't talking to each other. The suit was making friends with a double vodka on the rocks, and the cowboy had a headless draft going flat in front of him, and he was writing in a little book. He wrote with a yellow pencil covered with tooth marks, and I was reminded of fifth grade when I used to bite my pencils just so they'd be really mine.

I stood there for a while, ignored, which is not something I'm used to, sipping my drink. The suit finished his vodka, and Jamie, who keeps watch to see that his patrons are refilled right up to the legal BAC, appeared. The suit nodded, and Jamie gave him another.

Cowboy didn't even look up. Jamie and I exchanged glances, and I winked, so he asked me about another Appletini though I still had an apple ring afloat. I said a few things to Jamie, the usual banter, and Cowboy finally took note.

He had eyes I'd pay to drown in, a scar like a lightning bolt on his cheek, and the whitest teeth I'd seen off of a magazine page. "Goes down easy," he said to the bartender nodding in my direction.

When Jamie said, "Those sweet ones do," and nodded in my direction, too, I took in a quick breath. I was still off balance, but then I realized they were talking about the Appletini, and I murmured, "And anyway I'm not all that sweet." I knew what I was saying.

Cowboy looked at me, holding the pencil in his teeth the way a cartoon pirate holds a dagger when he swings on a rope to board a victim's ship. He smiled around the pencil. I was waiting for him to say, "Sure you are, Sugar," but instead he took the pencil out of his mouth and said, "Used to smoke."

"I heard you still do," I said, and put my glass on the bar near his beer. "Or was that just a pleasant rumor?"

"Refresh?" he asked. You knew he kept drinking company, the way he said that.

When Jamie brought my new drink, I poked the apple slice floating on top of it and licked off my finger. "Makes you think you're drinking something healthy," I said.

"Life's all about illusion," he said, and I told him I knew just what he meant. I tried to get a look at his notebook, and I saw ragged lines that might be poetry, but I couldn't make out any words, and he folded the book closed and put it into his pants pocket. He couldn't be casual about that since he had to stand up to do it, and, when he stood, I didn't step back and neither did he, so we were as close as if we'd been slow dancing. Even in the bar I could tell he smelled like fresh-cut grass.

I fed him the slice of apple floating on my drink and, though he wouldn't switch to Appletini's, he liked it each time I lifted that dripping slice, folded it, and fed it to him with my sweetened fingers.

It took until last call before he called me "Sugar," and, fuck, if Jamie wasn't right.

Turns out Cowboy isn't a poet, or if he is, he's the first one I've met who hasn't made me listen to him read his rhymes at me. I told him my name, but all night he kept calling me Eve, and even though I asked him, he never would say why.

Just Another Sack

VICKI TAKES HIS MEASURE from across the room, watches him lean on the bar and scan the room with his eyes. He's big, some would say fat. She likes that in a man, makes her feel fragile in the arms. She's stringy and tough, likes the feeling of being girly.

If he were closer she'd check out his hands. Her mama taught her that: hands tell all, see how he treats the waitress. That's how he'll treat you. Should of listened to mama, she thinks, running her thumb up the edge of her blouse, tucking in her bra strap.

Jet black hair, eyes the color of a husky. He's looking at her over his drink. She heads out to the ladies room, picks a stall.

Vicki's sure there's another way, but she doesn't know it. She goes into a stall, takes off her panties, and lies on the floor, the gray tile cold under her back, and props her feet up on the wall of the stall opposite the roll of toilet paper. She inserts a female condom and a tube of Koromex jelly. Nobody's going to stick his mouth there tonight.

Bob had never used protection — and she hadn't either. But in eleven years no kids. So whose fault was that? Can't feel hardly anything with the condom in. The jelly makes the condom less obvious. Juicy pussy.

Back at the bar, he offers a drink. She wants bourbon on the rocks, smiles and asks for bourbon and soda, more ladylike. Too late for white wine. She smiles, tries to hide her teeth.

She's on the wrong side of thirty-five, she thinks, and this is no long slide. More tilt-a-whirl these last few years. His eyes keep scanning the room the whole time they talk. She turns and looks over her shoulder, and then he says he'll take her home.

Fine with her. Mr. Big, with jet-black hair, says his name is Jack. Sure. Jack. Jack Black, Jack Daniels, don't know jack, Jack be Nimble. Yeah, Jack, be nimble. Jack and the Beanstalk. Let's see your magic beanstalk, Jack. Later?

His hands tell the tale, smooth, no ring mark, neat nails, clean, not jagged. They won't tear her up if he gets friendly.

He drives fast. She explains the kids are hungry — gives them the names of her favorite characters in *Days of Our Lives*. He'll never know. They never do. Kids keep the men out of her house, keeps it uncomplicated.

Last year she didn't follow her rule. Couldn't get one of them out of her house. Shit, couldn't get him out of her pussy. By the time he left she was all torn up. No more. No, four children keep the men out of her house, not out of her.

She points to a house, says it's empty, and the back porch has a swing. They go round and he gets on her, in her. She looks up and over his shoulder at the peeling paint on the ceiling, feels the swing's slats against her back. They move, the swing's chains creak, and she can't hardly feel a thing. Maybe he's smaller than she thought he'd be. Maybe it's the condom. No wonder men griped. Don' wanna wear one, can't feel. Shit. They were right.

So she can't feel his dick. Still, let him think he's a good fuck. He gave her a ride, now she'll give him one. Move your hips, she tells herself, say baby baby, Jack be nimble, say you're so fine. Thrust. Move. Dig your fingernails into him, but don't break a nail off. Moan. Come on, now. "Ride me, Jack."

Vicki would give him more of a show, but he's quick, this one, like a rabbit. In and out a couple dozen times, just enough friction to let her know he's been there.

She watches him drive away, burning rubber. She's carrying her shoes in her hand along with her purse. She walks barefoot across the lawn, the grass cool and damp under her feet. She turns the key in the door of the empty house.

Stone

As I remember, I tried to tell myself it was just a day-trip, requiring only a stop at the ATM for an extra twenty. Since I knew where we were going, it was pointless to look for a map. Besides, I took pride in knowing how to travel light, and until then I'd gotten away with it.

"You look great," Steve said.

I clutched the bouquet I'd bought at Whole Foods, yellow chrysanthemums and a few white carnations with some greenery.

"You're still blonde," he said, grinning.

I thought about his old jokes about bottle blondes, and tried not to wince. "You do too," I said. He looked like a doctor in a TV commercial: straight-backed, smiling, sleek and silver. Marriage agreed with him. I always knew it would.

He was in town for a conference. He'd phoned to suggest we get together and visit both sets of parents. In fact, we were visiting their graves: they themselves were long gone.

Of course, they weren't in the same cemetery. His were in Beth Israel, mine in Calvary. I hadn't been to Beth Israel for at least ten years, though I passed it on the regular visits I made to what I thought of as my cemetery.

"Rock-scissors-paper for who goes first?" he'd said.

I shook my head. "Yours first."

I was surprised again at how shiny the black granite headstone was, how imposing. Off to one side, a privet had grown around and over a small bench where once we might have sat. I wondered at the decision of the landscaping crew, which had pruned the hedge flat so that the bench occupied a neat, snug niche.

His parents had bought two extra plots: for Steve and his wife, though he'd had no wife when the plots were purchased. I'd wondered if he'd use them, come so far for this, and if he did, would I know?

My parents had done the same as his. I'd have the luxury of sprawling sideways across both plots, like a woman sleeping alone in a double bed.

Steve reached into his pocket and pulled out a stone, white and smooth as an egg. He placed it on the headstone. He pulled out another, and handed it to me: carnelian. I held it in my palm and rubbed it with my thumb.

"Beautiful," I said, then set it next to his. I stared at the two stones together, and my eyes filled with tears. I hoped he'd think my tears were for his parents or my own.

I waited while he read from a little blue book.

Not long afterwards, we stood at my parents' grave. I didn't blame them now, any more than I blamed his. We'd been adults. I set the bouquet at the foot of the stone. "I don't say prayers here," I said, though he hadn't asked. I counted to one hundred, and pretended it was reverential silence.

Waiting for him today, I'd felt the same rising anticipation I'd had before my first visit to the cemetery, as though I'd expected my father to be sitting there, reading a paper, a lit cigarette hanging from his mouth, with a glass of beer going flat and warm beside him, and, though interrupted, he'd be glad to see me. By the time my mother died, I knew better, made the visits from love and duty.

We stood in front of my steps.

"Are you sure you'll be all right?" he asked.

"Sure," I said. It was the right, the only, answer.

"Well, then," he said and kissed me on the cheek. He squeezed my arm just above the elbow.

I wondered if he was thinking about the bandage the phlebotomist had left. He hadn't asked me about it, or about anything else significant.

"Take care," he said.

He might as well have said, "Have a nice day."

Then he got back into his rental car. Before he pulled away, I called out to him, wishing I could instead ask the question I'd been sucking like a lozenge.

The wind blew away his inconsequential answer, and he was gone. I fumbled with my keys, grateful it was only the deadbolt I had to unlock. There'd be a cairn formed over the years if all the visitors to a grave left a stone. And if caretakers removed each little stone, what did they do with it, what could anyone do with a stone?

Good Company

DON'T GET ME WRONG, I'm no prude, but sometimes no means no. I like to think I can take care of myself, but I've been roughed up a couple times, nothing serious, just a few bruises.

No one believes me when I tell them I'm thirty-seven, but it's the truth. I was thirty-seven on November 19. You can ask my friend Carol. She'll tell you.

Carol would tell you whatever I asked her to tell you. We do that for one another. You know how it is. A woman goes out for a few drinks, meets a man, wants him to know some things, doesn't want him to know others. Mostly I don't need her help.

Like I said, sometimes no means no, and sometimes it doesn't. Some men, they like a woman who's a challenge. Others, they're in a rush, or they want a woman who's not afraid to say "yes", even "yes, please". I only say "please" when I know I'll get what I want.

The trick is telling who wants what.

I don't go to a bar unless I want it. I could drink at home cheaper — and wear comfortable shoes besides. I have good legs, the kind men say don't stop. So I wear high heels when I go out, four inches at least. My feet kill me.

I don't have all that much on top, but I don't sag neither. I pass the pencil test if you know what I mean.

I'm a good five foot ten in heels.

You go to a bar after work, have a few drinks, meet a man who had a few drinks. Maybe one of you wants to get laid, maybe you both do. Like I said, I don't go to a bar unless I want it.

Don't get me wrong, I have standards. His fingernails have to be clean, he has to treat the waitress nice, and he has to tell me his name before we have a drink.

And he has to remember my name, which I tell him right away. That's after he's made the first move, of course.

I like to look a man in the eye when I'm drinking with him. If we make it, I don't have to look him in the eye, I know what's what.

Just because I'll fuck a man I just met doesn't mean I'm crazy. I take care of myself, use one of them female condoms, which aren't cheap. I spend more on condoms than I do on nylons. I've never had sex worth dying for.

I won't make the obvious joke about dying for it. Don't get me wrong, but sometimes I wish my standards weren't so high.

Some nights I go out by myself. I don't have anyone to look out for me, but I don't have to worry about anyone neither.

With Carol, we have a deal that we leave with each other or not, depending on what happens. And we have signals so that if one of us gets stuck, we get the other out. If one of us is talking to a guy for a long time, if she puts on lipstick, it means, get me out of this.

It's kinder that way than blowing a guy off, don't you think?

Nobody who's going out planning to get laid has a right to expect the truth. That includes me. I'd like to find Mr. Perfect, but what are the chances of that, you tell me.

When I married Bob I thought he was Mr. Perfect—and I thought I would be Mrs. Perfect and we'd have Baby Girl Perfect and Baby Boy Perfect.

We didn't.

So after eleven years one day he looks at me and says, "Elvis has left the building." You want to know something? I didn't have to ask what he meant.

I got the house and the rest of the mortgage and he got the car and the bank account. I have the wedding album which neither of us wanted. It seems, well, wrong to just toss it in the garbage bin.

So when I went out last night, I wasn't expecting to meet Mr. Perfect. If I ever think I have met him, I'll sober up before I wonder whether he'd wear a wedding band even when I'm not there.

About last night, in case you're wondering: I did.

If graphic sex embarrasses you, please stop reading here.

Like I said, nobody believes I'm thirty-seven. I think it's because I'm so thin. Or maybe the lights are dim. Whatever.

Mark was smooth, slow. When we were on the way to my place I lied and said I had a roommate who would be back.

First thing we were in the house, I took off my shoes. I knew he wasn't going to leave until we'd fucked.

Later I was sorry I hadn't told the truth.

Mark kind of guided me so I was on top. Usually if I'm on top, I'd feel like I was in control, but not with him. Partly because it wasn't my idea. And then it was that he moved me around, pulled me down so he was deep inside, deep as anyone could be, and we both came, me first and third, and I collapsed onto him.

I was sweating and so was he. Afterwards he found a couple of his hairs on my chest. He picked them off me and made a predictable joke. We both laughed.

Laughing like that I almost forgot what we were doing together.

Anyway just because he's good in bed doesn't mean he'd be a good lover or a good husband. I told myself that when he left without writing down my phone number.

Still, I got what I wanted, didn't I?

Score

ALL SHE CARED ABOUT was that he was late again. Bobbie sat at the counter, her coffee cold and bitter.

"Can you beat this?" the waitress asked, holding up the day's paper and pointing to the headline.

"Don't know of much worse," Bobbie said, "shaking a helpless baby like that." Even as she spoke she knew she was lying, and she didn't care.

"For pity's sake," the waitress said, "the mother's defending the bastard."

"Go on, she's not?" Bobbie said, knowing how women stayed, made excuses for every behavior if they were getting it when and how they needed it.

"He's got post-traumatic syndrome," she read, "that's what the mother says, and the baby's crying set him off. I don't believe her, do you?" the waitress asked, not waiting for an answer.

"Jan" was the name on her uniform.

"Kitchen'll be closing soon, Hon, if you'll be wanting something to eat."

"Little warm-up on the coffee maybe, Jan, if you don't mind."

"My pleasure, should've noticed you were running low."

Nothing here seemed real in the fluorescent light.

"Open the paper these days," the waitress said, "all you see is bad news spread out all through, from page one even to the comics and classifieds, not to mention sports — and how long has it been since we've had a winning team anyway — and real estate, you'd think that at least would be what you call cheerful, new starts and all, but instead what you get is sink holes swallowing up rows of homes and new developments cancelled because the landfill they're built on has been labeled, like, toxic."

"Poor planning," Bobbie said, "is at the heart of it all."

"Quiet out there, ain't it?"

"Raining, so everyone's tucked in at home."

"Seems like it. Take only a minute, and I can run through a fresh pot for you."

Until then Bobbie had been renting her stool at the counter, paying tips in her mind for each cup. Victor could've picked a better place for her to wait, someplace with real tables and good chairs, maybe even a candle on the table.

"Who you waiting for, Hon?" the waitress asked, then caught Bobbie's expression and her trembling hands gripping the cup, and she backed away. X: with two black lines of magic marker she crossed the day off the calendar, then turned around to Bobbie to say she didn't mean nothing by the question.

"Your guess is as good as mine," Bobbie said, "'cause I'm not sure I know who he is any more, which is something I'm sure you know just what I mean."

Zippers, thought Bobbie, is what I need: one to keep my mouth shut, one to unzip Victor's heart so he's on time so I don't get sick any more, one for my grave to keep it closed until I need it, and one to open the sky so I can see who or what's up there keeping us going, which was the closest she'd come to a prayer since, well, the last time Victor was late.

Ferret Anxiety

YOU OPEN YOUR EMAIL, skim the senders and subjects. You see a subject line "ferret anxiety." You don't recognize the sender. So? You didn't recognize cutiepie10018, either, and that was your college roommate. Does this email explain how to tell when a ferret is anxious, or offer help for anxious ferrets, or does it describe a new syndrome named ferret anxiety?

Although you are, have been, anxious for a long time, nonetheless you are puzzled. Your anxiety has been diagnosed as free-floating. Until now, your anxiety had nothing to do with ferrets, although you are certain you wouldn't want one as a pet, nosing about in crevices and corners where it has no business.

You click ferret anxiety for a preview. The message is unintelligible. You remember, "What's the frequency, Kenneth?," which remains an unsolved puzzle. The scattered words in this mail and the numbers make no sense to you. You ask yourself why you have been singled out to receive this coded message. You believe that if you ignore it, some disaster will befall you or those you love, perhaps the entire country — frogs, boils, hail, locusts, darkness, death of the first-born. All these will come to pass even more surely than if you had failed to send along a chain letter.

You ask yourself repeatedly, "What is ferret anxiety?" Quick hairy snakes, ferrets are, with legs. You shudder thinking about a ferret, lurking, and what was it you saw just now, a swift shadow on the floor?

For weeks you will murmur the phrase "ferret anxiety." Your friends will overhear you, watch you jerk your head to catch clear sight of the fleeting movement near your feet. You see it many times a day. You dare not try to explain. Finally, you understand.

Girl Waiting

NIDA LOOKS at the email subject line, "Very Sweet Girl Waiting," and wonders why this Gutierrez is writing to her. She has been editing so long that she thinks for a moment of replying to Gutierrez to tell him he should change the subject line to "Sweet Girl Waiting."

Gutierrez sits at a rough plank table, a half-empty bottle of red wine next to a clear tumbler. The label on the bottle is stained with wine. Gutierrez pours carelessly. Perhaps he is also thinking of the girl, or he may be in a hurry to fill his glass.

"It's you," he says to Nida. His voice suggests neither surprise nor pleasure. He raises his glass and offers it to her, a nasty smile on his face. He knows she will not drink from his glass.

Nida looks around. She doesn't see a computer. A newspaper, folded in thirds, lies on the table. Gutierrez opens the paper and reads. Nida stands behind him, but, although she sees the headlines, she can't understand the language. The photographs are blurred as though they'd been taken from a moving bus.

"You want something?" he asks without raising his eyes from the paper.

A candle gutters below a naked light bulb that swings on a cord from the ceiling. The windows are closed on newspaper to keep out cold air. The windows have not been opened for a long time, and the newspaper is yellowed. A fire hazard, Nida thinks. She worries about the girl who is not at the table with Guitterez, but locked in the next room. Gutierrez, in danger, would take care of himself leaving her to perish. Has an earthquake shaken the building, causing the bulb to swing?

Nida shakes her head. She recognizes Gutierrez from the 42 bus, which she takes to work in the morning.

Gutierrez has not shared his wine with the girl. Nida can see her sitting on a faded armchair. The arms of the chair are threadbare. The girl rests her head against a white crocheted antimacassar.

In the girl's room, a 60-watt bulb is screwed into a metal starburst in the ceiling. The walls swallow the light, like a hungry dog swallowing a scrap.

The girl rests, and in her lap, her hands lie still, one in the other, her tapered fingers curling towards her belly. Her pale eyelids are closed. Nida would like to see the girl's eyes. The girl's lips curve up. Nonetheless, Nida sees she is not smiling. She has a dolphin-like mouth that gives her face the look of perpetual pleasantness. Nida has no patience with these mouths or their owners, who have deceived her. She will not make that mistake again. Through her irritation, she tells herself the girl has done nothing to harm her. Can do nothing?

No, she remains sitting, eyes closed. A narrow bed with a black metal headboard is pushed into a corner. A khaki blanket covers the bed. A thin white pillow lies in the center of the bed. Why? Nida scans the room. No mirror hangs over the scarred bureau on which a red plastic pocketbook sits gaping. A pale-yellow silk scarf hangs out of the bag like the tongue of a sick man. Nida reminds herself that looks are deceiving.

Back in the room with Gutierrez, Nida sees that the light bulb has come to equilibrium. Nothing in the room is in motion, not even Gutierrez himself. He is not breathing, but he is not dead.

Locked in the next room is the very sweet girl. Nida has Gutierrez' word, and he has no reason to mislead her. What is she waiting for? For whom? Her computer has gone to sleep. She pours a glass of wine from the bottle with the stained label. A sweet girl.

Vile

LATER SHE WAS FORCED to admit that she knew what she was doing. She cast aside her mask of virtue.

She has to confront herself, to see her image as she herself has drawn it: her cheeks flushed, her lips swollen, her breasts tipped with puckered aureoles and hardened nipples. There on the page she can see that her dark, curling pubic hair is damp with unconsummated desire for him. Perhaps she will tell him how her own clever fingers open her body to spasms of pleasure.

She dresses to please him, to know that when she writes about the clothing she has chosen, she will hear from him an echoing intake of his breath because her clothing is for neither warmth nor comfort. She lifts it from hangers, removes it from its tissue in the drawer only if it will have some value to this game she plays, in which his arousal and his satisfaction become her great prize.

So she chooses shoes in which she cannot walk except for his amusement. These four-inch heels reshape the calf muscles of her leg. He likes watching her walk, knowing she cannot run away from him in these shoes. She would not run away from him even if she could run. Tonight when she writes how she would like to pleasure him, she will leave her shoes on. She will tell him how he will feel the sharp points of the heels on the backs of his thighs when he is inside her. She will tell him that if he listens carefully, he can hear the click of her heels when she wraps her legs around his waist.

She wraps a long blue paisley silk scarf around her neck. She will leave it on after all her other clothes lie in a heap on the floor where they will stay until she has written everything else. She will write to him to remind him that she stands naked in front of him, wearing only her high-heeled black sandals and her scarf. She will ask him to watch as she unwinds the scarf from her neck. She holds one end high above her head in front of her body and she reaches down so that she can slide the scarf back and forth between her legs. She looks for the right words to describe the silken pressure moving over this place so sensitive to touch, to the caress of his watchful gaze, to her own words. She no longer knows if her words are meant only to entice him, or whether they are designed to tease her until she yields again.

She knows he will read this and wonder if moments after she stopped writing she gave herself the pleasure she wrote about, and if so, then was she was really thinking of him?

Convictions

EVEN WITH THE LIGHTS OUT Lucy could see the pale scar like an accent circumflex on Sloan's upper lip. It was not more than a quarter of an inch from point to point. Still, as he hovered over her, it was the scar she saw, not his face, as first he watched her intently and then gradually withdrew into his own climax. No, through it all, she saw only the scar.

She herself had a scar on her left hand, cut by a broken drinking glass into which, palm down, she'd been forcing an ice cube. She saw her own scar as a record of her personal history, a mark of foolish persistence. She was sure Sloan's scar was a hieroglyphic notation of his past.

She waited until they'd grown close enough for her to trace it with her finger before she asked him about it. He told her that when he was sixteen a girl had thrown a rock at him. And now he had the scar. He hadn't wanted to say more to her, and Lucy noticed the muscle in his jaw clench as it did when he was unhappy.

The time came, as it always does for two newly in love, to trade childhood stories. She told him how when she was four the older neighborhood kids had sent her out onto the fishpond to test the ice — and how they'd brought her home, drenched and shivering, to her outraged parents. And she told him how when she was twelve, she and the boy next door had used the can of gasoline from a lawnmower to dribble a trail of gas across the backyard and light it. Somehow they'd gotten away with that, and, she'd hinted, more.

In return Sloan told Lucy that he'd made explosives with his chemistry set and detonated them in the back of his house in the winter. He liked to see the snow fly up. And he told her how he'd made a substitute teacher cry by setting off explosives like cherry bombs, disrupting classes she'd barely had under control anyway. And later he told her how he'd set off little explosions in his living-room fireplace when his parents were gone.

Because of her own experience with the gasoline, Lucy found none of his stories daunting. After all Sloan hadn't tortured small animals or practiced self-mutilation.

Besides, Lucy knew herself to be what was once called a strong-minded woman. She had opinions, and after a while those opinions developed for her the force of documented fact.

In her eyes Sloan's greatest virtue was that he seemed to be blind, or at least indifferent, to her allegiance to her convictions. Although she knew he valued what he called "loyalty," Lucy never thought that Sloan might have conjectured that her convictions about his worth would serve his purposes.

Sloan's indifference to Lucy's list of unassailable convictions, this virtue, was insufficient in itself for a relationship, but there was enough superficial compatibility for them to become, in the manner of so many other young people like them, a couple.

Lucy learned that Sloan valued loyalty and had punished slights. In high school he stole the notebooks of classmates who snubbed him, so they would do poorly on their exams. After a girl had refused to dance with him at an eighth-grade party, he stole her cat and took it to the animal shelter as a stray. Of course Lucy had not heard these things at once, or even in the first year of their going together.

Lucy watched almost with detachment as first Sloan left a toothbrush, then underwear and shirts in her apartment. But she almost held her breath as more and more of his belongings took possession of her apartment. Her bureau became their bureau, and her closet, their closet. He began to call in the afternoon to say when he would be home.

It wasn't until he'd given up his apartment and they were "indissoluble," as he said, that she chanced to ask again about his scar. This time he told her more, how he'd been riding his bike and Sandy DeMarco, who lived a few streets away from his home, had taken aim as if he were a moving a target in an arcade, had hurled a rock, and hit him in the face. She knocked him off his bike, and left him lying in the street. He had nearly been run over while she hid in her house.

"Why did she do that?" Lucy asked with the proprietary tone of a woman whose man has been wronged.

He shrugged. "She just felt like it, I guess."

"Didn't you ever find out?"

"Why bother."

"What did you do to get even?" The question came naturally. Knowing him as he was, she was sure that he wouldn't have let this pass without retribution.

Sloan's face was blank, so neutral that only concentration could have emptied it so completely of any trace of emotion. "I didn't have to do anything," he said. And then his expression changed to what it always was when he spoke of how he'd "done things," bright and matter-of-fact. "I didn't have to," he repeated.

"You didn't have to?" What a funny way of putting it, she thought. "Why not?"

"The next week her little brother died, was killed, in a freak accident. Apparently he'd found some explosives, probably from a construction site, people thought, and he'd bit them or something."

"How could that be?" Lucy watched him look past her.

"I don't know. I was a kid. It was in the papers. We talked about it at school. That's all."

70

She felt his eyes search her face for another question, a sign of insistence, of disloyalty. She had her suspicions, her ideas, what would eventually become for her a conviction. Because it must remain unspoken there could be no denial, no appeal, only a long sentence of silence for both of them, and, of course, the scar.

Hag

THE DAY Sean told her that he was moving out was the day he dug his video camera out of the box of stuff that he'd kept in the back of the closet. They'd never set it up on a tripod and aimed it at the bed. They'd never taken it to the shore or anywhere else. It had always stayed in the box, loaded.

Now he aims it at Anna as she paces around what had just become her bedroom again. She's crying, and she's been crying off and on for hours while Sean packed. Her face is red and swollen with grief and anger. Her long, gray hair falls into her face and sticks where her face is wet with tears and snot.

The bed is a staging area between them. Sean's belongings and clothes cover the bed in heaps. He hasn't started putting things into suitcases yet. A six-pack of cartons from Staples leans up against the bed.

The Kleenex is on the same side of the bed as Sean, and Anna won't go there. She wants him to stop the camera. She grabs a shirt from the pile of clothes and holds it up, open like a curtain in front of her face. "Stop," she says, from behind the shirt, and then says it again, "Stop it." She's sobbing, "Don't. You have no right." She lowers the shirt and he's still filming.

"No...." her voice trails into a whimper. She hates melodrama, hates being out of control.

"Erase it! Erase it now!" She's begging though the words are commands. Later she will not remember what else she said.

"Look," he says. He presses some buttons, watching the monitor, and then he turns the screen towards her. She sees herself reduced, holding up the shirt and hears herself say it in a tinny voice, "Stop, Stop it. Don't. You have no right. No...Erase it. Erase it now."

She sees herself, diminished, lower the shirt, and the zoom-in close-up of her face. She sees herself as he will remember her and as she will remember herself, like this: her hair wild, her face puffy and streaked, bags under her tiny red-rimmed eyes.

Anna's mouth opens and closes like a ventriloquist's dummy's when Sean turns off the sound.

Niagara

IT WOULD BE GOLDILOCKS WEATHER ALL WEEKEND, and Dan suggested driving on over to Niagara Falls. They could get a room on the Canadian side, he was sure.

They were nearly there when he said he wanted to fuck her. No surprise. After all he'd suggested they go to one of the honeymoon capitals of the world, and they weren't even married. Holly didn't expect that they were going to spend the night watching reruns of Andy of Mayberry on Classic TV.

For nearly a year he'd been sending mixed signals. Now he told her that he'd wanted her for a long time, that he could hardly keep his hands off her, that he wanted to wrap his fingers in her hair and pull her face to him. All the time he spoke, he kept his hands on the wheel and his eyes on the road. He was, she said to herself, a safe driver.

"You mean a lot to me, Holly," he said. "That's why I have to tell you that I won't be making love. This would be a no-strings-attached fuck."

Holly considered grabbing the wheel and turning it sharply. Maybe then he would look at her. On either side of them, the dirty silver sides of semis loomed. They were in a moving tunnel.

"So, what about it?" He turned to glance at her.

"Let me think about it, Dan." Now that it was her turn she studied the highway stretching ahead of them. She'd worn a black velvet pullover and the perfume she'd worn when he'd kissed her all those other times. If she hadn't wanted to sleep with him, she wouldn't have said yes to the trip, but this wasn't what she'd had in mind. She wasn't traveling to Niagara Falls only to be made in the mist. But then she said, trying to keep the panic out of her voice, "You brought condoms, right?"

And was it because he'd not wanted to seem cocksure that he hadn't brought condoms? Or was he just all out of them and hadn't had time to swing by the drugstore at home? Holly hadn't committed herself to anything, but said he should buy condoms anyway. "They don't go bad soon," she said, adding in a flat voice, "if we don't need them, I'm sure you'll find a use for them."

So they drove around and discovered which drugstores in Niagara Falls, Canadian side, closed at nine. Most of them. Finally they found one just a few minutes before closing time. And while Dan went into the store, Holly stayed in the car.

Holly opened her pocketbook and dug out her cell phone. She clutched it and peered through the windshield of the car and then through the plate-glass window of the store waiting for a glimpse of him in line. She wondered how much a call to her therapist in Great Neck would cost. She knew that the therapy bill to fix the fallout from her decision—whatever happened—was sure to dwarf the cost of the call. Holly imagined Dan's return, and explaining, "Oh, just having a little chat with my therapist trying to decide whether or not to fuck you tonight." She put the phone back in her purse.

Still, she told herself, this is better than the love-you-love-you-not that she'd been getting. This time the message was clear: a simple fuck. Niagara Falls, but no hearts and flowers.

As he appeared at the drugstore door, the lights of the store went out behind him. Dan held a small brown bag in one fist. He was beaming, and in his other hand he carried aloft, as though it were a torch, a single long-stemmed rose.

Hay

IN HOT HUMID WEATHER the buffet drawers had a tendency to stick. Lou had promised to wax the runners back in June. He'd promised to do a lot of things in June. And May. And April. July had come and gone. It was dead into August. He grabbed the wooden knobs and pulled hard. The drawer that had been filled with ironed white linens and embroidered tablecloths was almost empty. Settled on a folded worn bath towel were two .38's like birds in a nest.

Lou stood for a long time and stared down into the drawer. Anyone watching would have thought that he hadn't left them there himself, hadn't loaded them three weeks ago, ignoring all rules of safe gun storage. Any teenager looking for a stash of silver to sell for drugs could have found these and done who knows what sort of damage. Lou had heard the warning voice in his head, but had left them loaded anyway. Hell, every kid from town would know not to try to rob this place, not now, not when everything worth more than five dollars had been moved into town in a big rented U-Haul truck back in July.

Lou checked to see that the safety lock on the guns had been set, and he tucked each of them into his belt in back. No sense taking chances now.

He went into the kitchen, his footsteps echoing in the nearly empty rooms. On the counter was his ex-wife's pottery mug — the one with the rosebud. Technically, Kay wasn't his ex yet, but since she'd moved in with Chuck, Lou hated thinking of her as his wife.

She'd moved out, leaving the dishwasher running. Funny, the things women do, he'd thought when he came home and found the house emptied, except for a few pieces of furniture and the load of dishes drying in the Maytag. "If that don't beat all with a stick," he'd said aloud.

If they'd had kids, he would have called his son to say, "You'll never guess what your mother's gone and done now."

He found the old honey-do list on the kitchen table. On the bottom, Kay had scrawled, "My phone number's on the fridge, the card for Chuck's TV and Small Appliance Repair. But don't come looking."

As if he would. Confusion gave way to disbelief and then, to anger, and finally to a misery so profound it was numbing. But that was July. And this was August.

He hefted the mug. He'd considered smashing it with a hammer and then taking the shards and leaving them in a small bag on Kay's doorstep, or mailing them to her. But he wasn't sure if that violated some federal law. He'd even considered making a trip to town and returning the mug to her in person, saw himself standing on the porch, freshly shaved and showered, his hair slicked back with Vitalis. What could be the harm in that? She had, after, all told him where she was. He had called a few times, sheepish, making one excuse or another, and she'd been at least polite, until the last call when he heard Chuck muttering in the background. Then she'd been as eager to hang up as if he'd been cold calling to ask her to buy aluminum siding.

A bottle of Wild Turkey stood on the kitchen table. He poured what was left into the mug. Through the window over the sink he could see the field, the hay cut last week, rolled this week. He looked at the hay rolls, and, out of habit, at the sky checking for rain, knowing already that no rain would come tonight or tomorrow or even the next day after that.

The air was thick. A cloud of gnats flew a few inches from his face as he walked out in the stifling evening. He carried the mug in one hand as he walked, careful not to trip over the deep ruts the tractor had made. He remembered the big haystacks of his youth where he and his brother had played. And the hayloft in the barn where he and Kay had lain together huddled that December night, looking through the roof he'd patch, thinking about those stars.

He walked out to the hay roll farthest from the house and lowered himself carefully to the ground. He took the .38's from his belt and laid them on the ground. He sipped the Wild Turkey, and watched the haze turn color in the setting sun. Two 38's, sometimes it paid to be ambidextrous, he thought, and the timing will have to be just right.

He leaned back against the roll. He could feel the hay through his tee shirt. He ran his hand over the prickly golden stubble on the ground. His hay would be fine. And, anyway, now it was nothing to him.

Journey

BECCA IS TIRED. It has been a long day's walk from where the train had left her, no real station, just a wooden platform with nothing around it but meadows and beyond the meadows tree-covered hills. She carries her new shoes in one hand and a small gray-striped suitcase in the other. She's happy she hadn't minded leaving so much behind. As it is, the suitcase is all she can manage.

The road here is not much more than ruts in the ground and white stone showing through where wagon wheels have worn away the grass. When she stops, she can hear water falling onto rocks. Might be, Becca thinks, that she could get something to drink there or could even stop a while longer and stand in the stream — if it is a stream she hears and not a swift-flowing river.

Such a river would be of no use to her.

Up ahead a pine grove shades the road, and then road vanishes in the woods. All Becca hears is the hum of her own blood in her head, the hum louder than the water rushing, louder than the thrush song, louder than the wind in the pine boughs. If the road ends here, then she is certainly lost, without hope of making it to the cabin before nightfall.

She reaches the grove and stands on the fallen brown needles that cushion the path. She will have to sit here and rest a bit. She spreads her striped skirt beneath her. Gradually she hears the wind again, and the water, and the hidden birds calling to one another, and then from the distance, through the trees, comes the deep voice of a man calling to his horses and the scree of a wagon carrying a heavy load.

She will be all right. She is on the road that leads somewhere. And if she doesn't reach the cabin before nightfall, well, she tells herself, that will be all right, too.

Just One

THE TIME CAME when most of her friends were, as she put it, "hitched." Jen got to be a bride's maid and grin for the pix. She was a bride's maid and wore a long pink dress. She was a bride's maid and wore a long pale blue dress. Once she was a bride's maid, and she wore a long black dress with a slit up the side. And the last time she was a bride's maid she wore a long white lace dress. That bride was nuts, Jen thought. Point was, her friends were each in a nest with a man.

They had Jen come by for brunch (eggs whipped up with cheese and baked to a poof) or for drinks (chilled white wine and brie or cheese in a crock). Each time Jen brought a wee house gift. She wore the bride's gift, some cheap gold charm or pin. She'd take a tour of the house and say, "Wow! What a great place you two have! Is that a real fire there or gas logs? Gas? It looks so real! Wow! A back yard, too! And that big swing set? When you have kids you'll be glad you have it." Her friends would blush, and Jen knew she'd be "Aunt Jen" in a year, two years tops, though not a real aunt, of course.

Her friends tried to fix her up. Jen would find a strange man there to sit with her — to make four or six (none of her friends had room yet for eight). Had he not been there she would have been the odd one, the third wheel (a trike) or a fifth-the spare you should keep in the trunk, she joked. But she was saved from the trunk-they'd dragged in a man to sit with her. "Don't you think he's nice/cute/smart/hot/sharp? I think he likes you," her friends would say. Of course the man said he'd call her for lunch the next week. No call came.

Her friends said, "It just takes one." Jen knew they were right. She'd had one man-and then she had the next and the next. The men left her, or she left them. Each time she'd set out, for what she vowed to be the last time, to find the right man. Oh, she knew in her heart that there was no such thing as the right man, just the right man for right now.

She tried ads. She was shocked at all the men who said they liked long walks in the rain. What that meant, she learned, was that they were too cheap to spring for a cab. And, worse, they were too proud to let her pay.

She tried the clubs. She died her light brown hair blonde, then red, then went jet black. She wore spike heels. She wore short skirts (she had good legs she could flaunt, her friends told her so). She pierced her ears. She was too old to pierce her tongue. And, oh, could she dance! Once she went to a rave, sprayed her hair pink and blue, and got called "Ma" by three boys who hit on her all at once. She laughed and left on her own.

At the clubs she heard, "Hey, babe, your place or mine?" The guys at clubs had no lines at all or lines that were lame. They talked sports, but just bitched when their team lost. She knew more sports stats than they did. And the men she met had no deep thoughts. Once she heard a man next to her at the bar say "Kant." She was all set to quote what she'd learned in Phil class in night school, but it turned out that he had not said "Kant," but the word she would not say that starts with C.

Yes, night school. She went there to learn-and to meet the right man. What she learned was that the course in Art was jammed with men, but not straight men. The man who sat next to her took her home in his cab, asked if she knew a nice guy for him. "Most men are such pigs," he said and winked. He said he'd call her for lunch, and he did.

She took a course where she learned to write what the prof called "pomes." He said free verse was frost with no net, or that's what Jen thought he said. She learned to rhyme and count beats. All the men there were too young or too old. None was just right. She felt like she was stuck in the tale with the three bears. Still when the course was done, she had a sheaf of "pomes." All that time with all those wrong men, those she'd dumped and those who had dumped her, all that time was good. She saw that now that she could write "pomes" to tell how her heart throbbed tears of blood. And the prof would write, "Nice work," "good tight lines here," and once when she dared write free verse, "great line breaks." She knew it had hurt him to write that. She was glad, for at first he had crossed out words and whole lines of her work. Her pomes had bled with his red ink that smudged and stained her hands and sleeves.

Jen did not have a man, but she could drink, dance and write "pomes." She found that she could drink and dance, but not dance and write or drink and write. And it cost much less to write than to drink or dance. Now when she went to her friends' homes, she did not bring wine, she brought her new "pomes." Of course she went out less and less. The right word was like the right man, worth the search. She looked for one at a time. Small words, short ones, like all of these.

An Old Story

THEY WERE AFRAID she would ruin him. Rhona was twice his age, but still he could drink legally anywhere.

In fact, they met at Rouge on a Friday after work when she left her credit card on the bar. The bartender called to her as she walked away, but she didn't hear in the noise. Jared picked up the card and squeezed through the crowd, calling her name, which he'd learned from her Visa. She offered to buy him a drink to thank him, thinking, "What a nice young man," and was pleased when he accepted.

They left Rouge to go to a less popular and quieter place only a few blocks away, and one thing led to another, and they stayed on for dinner. And Jared insisted on picking up the check, which left Rhona off-balance, because by the end of the dinner, she'd begun thinking, "What a nice man."

And when coincidentally Rhona and Jared ran on adjacent treadmills at the 12th Street gym the next morning, they laughed and agreed to go for lattes at Cosi after their workouts. They bought biscotti and stayed until lunch time.

That night Rhona was reading when the phone rang. It was Jared, violating the primary convention of single life, not to phone on a Saturday night. And the next morning they met for brunch at The Astral Plane. They sat in high-back wicker chairs under a parachute cloth ceiling and drank mimosas. She made a point of not telling him that she remembered when the restaurant had opened more than twenty years ago.

One thing led to another, and at dinner one night in the enchanted garden at Bump, where as breeders they were outsiders anyway, he called her darling. They drank two-dollar neon-blue Martinis all through happy hour, and she considered herself lucky. And when she was wobbly on 13th Street near the Historical Society she blamed the uneven brick pavement.

And they went to Moshulu, and sat on its deck drinking Long Island Iced Tea watching the pink of the sunset giving its glow to Camden. As they sat on the deck of a boat permanently moored between two bridges, watching the lights on the river, Jared said that before he was born he was in heaven waiting to meet her. And one thing led to another. In her bed he told her again and again that she'd spoiled him.

And before long she was picking up wine at the State Store. And shopping for two at the Reading Terminal Market. And making room for his clothes in her closet. And taking his clothes to the cleaners. And then doing all of his laundry. And then waiting at home while first he worked late and then later. And one thing led to another.

After all, they needn't have worried.

The Spell

JASON GNAWED ON HIS LOWER LIP; he was nervous, too. She'd worn a burgundy velour dress with a low neck, knowing she'd be overdressed. If Jason were going to be sitting for two hours, looking at her from the far side of an expanse of white tablecloth, she wanted him to have something to look at. He looked so handsome in his navy pinstriped suit.

The maitre d' led them to one of the tables in a row along a banquette. On one side sat a couple in their early sixties, about a decade older than Diane. On the other side two men, in their forties.

Diane was determined to be festive. She asked Jason to choose the wine, knowing that nothing on this menu would have notes of bubble gum and cotton candy. The worst that could happen would be a rosé.

Diane made a toast for Jason's birthday. As they were discussing the quality of the rack of lamb they'd ordered for dinner, they heard from one of the men say, "*Elle n'est pas son mère.*"

The two men continued *tout en français*. Diane had majored in French; Jason had just returned from two years in France working for Euro Disney. She flushed, watching his face evolve into a model of frustration.

And then Jason began to speak to her in perfect, rapid Parisian French. She answered in French.

The man sitting next to her switched to German to remark that it was amazing how many people spoke foreign languages these days.

The men leaned towards one another: nearly identical hair cuts, designer eyeglass frames, peach and aqua cashmere crewnecks worn over dress shirts. Their manicured nails gleamed in the candlelight. They might have been mannequins plucked from the window at L'uomo.

Diane understood.

The waiter brought course after course while the men served up pointed comments about Diane and Jason, who felt like specimens. Until that night they hadn't had a shared emotion other than their infatuation.

Later, in bed after they fell away from each other, they said, "*Elle n'est pas son mère.*"

For the next few years as they walked hand in hand, one would turn to the other and say the words, a spell to forestall the inevitable end.

Countdown for a Single Girl

EACH TIME CELESTE READ THE TEN COMMANDMENTS she checked to see which one she had broken most recently. Sometimes she had trouble deciding. The categories overlapped. Coveting. Adultery. Taking the Name in Vain.

Celeste could never remember the names of the players. It was the bottom of the ninth, the score tied, the bases loaded. She looked at the TV screen, and thought about Tom watching the game across town.

After her graduation from college eight years ago, Celeste attended a flurry of weddings. She watched carefree as bouquet after bouquet sailed over her head.

Sunday morning her cell phone rang at seven o'clock. Celeste wasn't expecting his call. She fumbled in her purse for the phone. Missed call. No message. His cell. She did not dare return the call.

Six months ago Celeste had already survived Christmas and New Years Eve. On Valentine's Day she went to dinner with three of her girlfriends. They drank Cosmopolitans and pretended they were only twenty-two, and they flirted with the Italian waiter, who looked at them as though he knew all their secrets.

Each time Tom left, Celeste told herself that in five minutes he would return, repentant, his mouth and hands stuffed with promises.

Tom came for supper. Celeste scrambled four eggs and topped them with sour cream and salmon roe caviar. She heated rolls in the oven. Just before he arrived, Celeste slipped a tiny spoonful of the translucent orange spheres into her mouth, pressed them with her tongue until her mouth filled with a burst of salty liquid.

Celeste and Tom and Jeannette. Three. Jeannette was always hovering, whispering, walking unexpectedly through the door of the coffee shop, her reflection fleeting besides theirs in shop windows.

Tom brought a bottle of champagne, cold from the liquor store, and two Waterford flutes to celebrate their anniversary.

In the morning one of the champagne flutes slipped from her hands and shattered on the tile kitchen floor. Struck by sunlight, the shards shimmered and glittered and glistened. In the center of the circle of broken crystal, Celeste stood barefoot and alone.

Just Like Other Girls

I HAD ARPEGE, but for the sake of friendship I wore the Jean Naté that Janet gave me for my birthday. We each kept a bottle of Jean Naté on our bureaus next to our lipsticks, Tangee Natural for school, Luvlee for going to the movies. Each of us also had a red lipstick and a stick of iridescent blue eye shadow. I used black eyebrow pencil to line my eyes, but Janet didn't.

At school we wore full skirts with many crinolines underneath. Some were net with a deep ruffle at the bottom. Usually we folded our white socks down over our saddle shoes, but some days we rolled our socks down to make fat white rings around our ankles. Most days I wore pink or white cotton blouses, though I had a blue dotted-Swiss blouse I liked better. Janet had a white organdy blouse. You could see her slip right through it and her bra straps too. You could see through the blue dotted-Swiss, but not as much. Janet wore a 32AA bra, and I wore a 34B.

We learned to dance in gym class. I spun Janet around and around. We had our special steps that we did, besides "side-together, side-together, back-step, back-step." When I danced cheek to cheek with Ira, Janet sat in the bleachers right where I could see her watching Ira twirl me and dip me until I said I was dizzy. Then I could sit with Janet. We were fifteen.

Date

HER HANDS WERE EVEN SMALLER THAN MINE. She pushed her tray along the stainless steel rails, and I followed, watching her square of red gelatin shimmy on its lettuce leaf. The cafeteria in the basement of the student center smelled of over-cooked Brussels sprouts and grilled meat. "Yellow Submarine" pulsed from hidden speakers.

The cashier looked at our meal plan tickets and nodded. We stepped out into an aisle and scanned the tables. Students from behind moved past us and around us to tables while we stood, holding our brown plastic trays of food. It took a long time, but we found a place.

"He didn't believe me," Dina said. Her lashes were long and spiky with tears. "I told him I was a virgin."

"Are you okay?" I asked. It was a stupid question, but everything I wanted to say was worse. I could feel my face burn.

She shook her head and looked down. That was enough for gravity to pull the tears from her eyes, and when she looked up again her cheeks were wet. "He thought I had my period when he saw the blood on the sheets in the morning. What did he think when he was trying to get his..."

She concentrated on slicing her skirt steak into tiny pieces, but she didn't eat them. She did this every night, cutting up all her food before she ate any of it. I'd grown used to it, but tonight it seemed like she was buying time. Hands in my lap, I dug my fingernails into my palms.

"I had to stay," she said as though I'd asked aloud. "He wouldn't take me home—it was too late to take the subway by myself."

"Too dangerous," I said. I knew she understood.

"It was," she answered.

90

"What are you going to do?"

"About what?"

She began to fork the food up to her mouth. She'd chew each piece for a long time and then sip some water. When she finished her meal we'd sit at the table until she burped—though I couldn't tell. Only then would she be ready to go. She'd blushed when, after weeks of eating together, she explained. Some nights she'd take a long time, and then she'd smile, and I knew she'd done it and we could leave.

"Everything," I said.

She shook her head, staring down at her plate. So that's the way it was. She made her mistake, and she's going to keep on making it. I'll stick with mine. Why not? I'd come here prepared to wait.

Twilight

"So," VERA SAID, "THAT'S THE WAY YOU WANT IT." She tugged at the chain of the lamp on the table next to her. They had been talking so long that dusk had seeped into every corner of the room. She knew her face would be puffy, her eyes red from crying.

Maxie stood behind the wing chair, her hands resting on the top of its back. The chair was between her and Vera. "I knew you wouldn't understand," Maxie said.

"Or like it?" Vera said. "There's a difference."

"I know more than you give me credit for knowing." Maxie walked around and sat in the chair. She stuck her legs out straight in front of her. She held her coat in her lap. The coat was a mound of brown tweed. Her purse was under the coat. She had been holding them the whole time.

"Tired?" Vera said. "You don't have to leave tonight."

"I don't have to do anything." Maxie said. "But, I do…"

"No, you don't. Not really."

Maxie hauled herself up out of the chair. "I'll get the rest of my things tomorrow, Vera, while you're at work."

"You think that will make it easier?"

Maxie nodded.

"On you or on me?" Vera asked.

"You're making it easier now," Maxie said. "On me."

"I never liked the way you fight with me," Vera said. "You have a way of putting me in the wrong."

"You're right, Vera."

"You're doing it again." Vera heard her own voice, querulous, raspy. She coughed, her chest rattling with congestion. It was the crying. "Go now if you want to go."

Maxie walked over to Vera and stood so close to her that Vera could smell Maxie's odor, like sour cabbage soup it was. Vera covered her face with her hands like a child playing peek-a-boo. She kept them there until Maxie walked away, until she heard the door open and close.

Crying made her cough. Tomorrow she'd look like she had a cold. That was a blessing. No one at work would have to know.

Armor

SIGNS OF LONG DROUGHT WERE EVERYWHERE. Leaves faded like an old photo left too long in the light. As I drove down the long, rutted dirt lane that led to their house, a shroud of dust rose behind me, and in the rear-view mirror I could see nothing else. When I pulled up to the house, Ann was leaning against the porch railing, while Burt sat across from her on a davenport. What had she told him?

Ann had changed as age and fashion had changed us all.

When Burt had gone, we stood like two women posing for a photograph we might find years later. She offered lemonade. A pitcher and three glasses waited on a small table. I imagined her strong hands applying themselves to the task of squeezing lemons, mixing sugar into the lemon and water, stirring until the liquid swirled. I hoped we would get past these civilities.

Burt paused in the doorway that was flanked by suits of armor, then stood watching us as Ann sat beside me. I asked about the armor. Ann said that it had come with the house, which had been an inn, that at first she would have paid to have someone take them away. They used to give her the creeps, but now she "couldn't think of this as home if they were gone. I wouldn't know what to do without them."

"They may be rusted on the outside," he added, "but inside, they're shiny and as good as new."

"Surely, you don't mean you wear them?" They glanced at one another and laughed as though this were an old joke, but I saw Burt and Ann confronting one another from within the suits. Worse, I felt the metal against my own bare skin, and I was suffocating, immobilized.

94

Exiled before dinner, I lay on the white chenille spread, watching the play of sunlight and the shadows of leaves on the curtains. While I waited to be readmitted to her world, I thought about the only time that Ann had acknowledged my feelings about her marriage.

The night she'd announced her engagement, she wore the ring that would become her wedding band. She hadn't said anything earlier while the others were with us. She'd waited until we were back in our narrow dormitory beds, lying in darkness. "I know you're against him," she said. "It doesn't make any difference; not to Burt, not to me."

She paused as though she expected me to deny it, although both of us would have known it was a lie. I gave her nothing she wanted then. And after a moment of my stubborn silence she said, "We can still be friends. It's up to you."

I closed my eyes, wanting her words to stop, wanting her voice to go on and on.

She said, "He isn't in the least cruel. He has a horror of cruelty."

I hadn't accused him of cruelty, but that night I dreamed Ann lay crumpled on the floor, as Burt stood over her, silent. She allowed him to pull her to her feet. Ann was small; she gave the impression of frailty. Only her strong hands with their blunt fingers and prominent veins suggested a woman who might be a match for this stranger.

Why had I come here? A hot, dry wind moved the curtains.

The next day Ann and I went out into the meadow that stretched between their house and woods. The woods dropped into a valley where Ann said we'd find a little stream, although the drought would have reduced it to a trickle of water over smooth stones.

In the slight stir of air the feathery tops of the grasses wavered, merging with the shimmer of heat. We moved through the scent of vegetation and dust. Branches and stalks brushed our bare legs. Ann

95

pointed out the thistles that had darkened to a deep purple. "Just a few weeks ago," she said, "they seemed eternal."

Once we had seemed eternal, too.

The sun caught in her hair. I wanted to reach out and trace the line of fire that was the tendril of hair at the nape of her neck. I held my hand back as though her hair might burn my fingers. "Are you happy, Ann?"

She looked up at me, eyes widened. Then she laughed, her only answer.

The days of the visit passed. We talked much, said little. The last evening after supper I started the dishes, expecting Ann to sit with me. Instead I felt him standing directly behind me. "I'll dry."

He took dishes from the drain board, dried them and lifted them onto shelves above the sink. I tried to concentrate on the warm soapy dishwater. We worked in silence.

Afterwards, I went out onto the porch where Ann sat. She looked up at me, "Finished?"

I could not find even a trace of irony. The empty, rusted shells stood sentinel. She pushed the soles of her feet against the porch deck, and the davenport moved, a creak filling the space where an answer might be.

That night, as if on cue, it rained. I lay listening to rain against the window, on the sill, on the red tin roof of the porch, rain drenching the leaves of the maple. In the morning the creek would be brown and swollen with run off. I lay, thinking about leaves hanging heavy with water, rain dripping from leaves, until, finally, I slept.

Ann stood by the car, stroking a fuzzy leaf of lamb's ear. "It was just like the old days," she lied.

Burt stood apart, chin up, staring off into the distance as I murmured my conventional answer. Then he turned and looked me in the eye. "Come again," he said. He might as well have taken my face in his hands. "Don't be such a stranger."

Maintenance

CHRISSIE WAS SUPPOSED TO BE HOLDING THE LADDER STEADY while I climbed. Instead she stood by its side and wrapped her arms around it in a big hug. My dirty sneakers were about her eye level when she sneezed with the kind of whole-body involvement she has with one of her better orgasms.

"Sorry," she said, "Sorry, sorry, sorry." She wiped the snot onto her bare arm up near her shoulder, and the ladder shuddered again.

The open can of white paint sat on the grass. I'd tucked the paintbrush and scraper into my belt for this first trip.

"It's OK, Kitten," I said, "I can come down. The windows can wait." The pear tree was in full bloom, a mass of pollen-spewing blossoms. I stayed where I was.

"I'll be OK," she said.

"Yeah," I said. "It's not you I'm worried about."

She looked up at me, her eyelids swollen and pink, her nose still running. "I said I was sorry," she said. Her voice had a kind of squeak to it.

I watched a big fat fly circle the ladder, spiraling down from over my head, down towards Chrissie's arm.

"Look. You know what I mean," I said.

Her only answer was to rub her nose on her shoulder again. Her blunt fingers curled around the wooden ladder. In the sunlight a trail of snot gleamed on her pale freckled arm like the path of a slug on a leaf. If I didn't think about it too long, it was sort of pretty.

Once Removed

ZERO TOLERANCE, LANA TOLD HERSELF, watching her husband Alex work the room. Yesterday she had considered leaving him if he made a fool of her again.

X's in her date book mark those occasions when she'd caught him doing something so blatant she felt humiliated by his failure to care enough to create a cover that might fool at least others, if not her. Watching him like this, Lana thought, showed how far she'd allowed herself to be pulled down.

Vince placed his hand on the small of her back, and she felt herself flush. Unless she was mistaken, Vince was less interested in her than he was in using her to stick it to Alex, who had included Vince's wife in his gaggle of women. That he'd slept with Regina was bad enough, but that he'd slept with her, then almost immediately taken others, was an insult Lana knew Vince had not forgiven.

Regina had forgiven him, however, or perhaps she'd never cared about sharing Alex; after all, she was sharing him with Lana. Questions about what Regina or the others cared about never bothered Lana. Perhaps they should have, she thought, if only to understand what lured Alex.

Open marriages had been fashionable when he had his first affair, and he'd tried to coax Lana into going along with it; she might have agreed had he not got a head start and been caught. Not that she had any desire to sleep with other men; Alex was enough man for her. Maybe his straying had taught him flexibility or sensitivity or just new moves that kept Lana from knowing what he'd do next in bed.

Lana amused herself by thinking she knew about what went on in the bedrooms of most of the guests at the party, thanks to Alex's bringing back to her what he'd got from his affairs, like a fond cat bringing its mistress a wounded mouse.

Kitchen capers, that's what he called it the first time he was caught.

Judy stared adoringly at Alex, brayed laughter at one of his witty comments and then looked over at Lana, who caught her eye and raised her glass in an ironic toast.

"I don't know what they see in him," Vince said, back at Lana's side and sounding like a petulant child, which gave Lana a glimpse of why Regina had been so easily distracted.

"He knows how to listen," Lana said, "or at least how to look as though he thinks you're the most charming person in the world — which makes him charming, of course."

"Good God, women still fall for that?"

"Fall they do, on their backs like Mistress Roundheels — or knees, whichever."

"Even after...everything, you make jokes?"

"Do you know why the chicken crossed the road?"

"Chicken?"

"Because Alex told her to."

Alex, she thought, was charming, really, could make her smile, would laugh at her jokes as though he thought they were funny even when he'd heard them before and she'd muffed the punch line, would never intentionally rub her nose in the mess he'd made, and then, too, she could smile because perhaps tonight she'd fuck Judy's husband, by proxy, and, of course, once removed.

Ridiculous

THE BASKET OF LAUNDRY was still warm from the dryer. A wisp of hair had fallen into my eyes, and I had no free hand to brush it out. I did that little puffing thing girls do in situations like this, trying to get the hair off my face, knowing it was futile but doing it anyway while Karl watched.

"You're being ridiculous," I said, setting the basket of laundry down near the bed.

"Am I, Donna?" he said. He leaned against the wall.

We have a routine with the laundry. Re-hang the towels in the bathroom, put the sheets and blankets on the bed, and then fold the rest of the laundry, dumping it on the just-made bed and folding or hanging from there.

"I think so." I bent into the basket and rooted around until I found the fitted bottom sheet. A pair of my panties and one of his socks clung to it like ornaments. I flicked them back into the basket, put the sheet on the bed in a white heap.

I looked at Karl. He hadn't moved. "Are you going to help me with this?" Even I could hear the irritation in my voice.

"I always do, don't I?" He took his place across from me and waited for me to hand him a corner. It usually takes us several tries to get the sheet properly oriented to go on the mattress. After the second or third try one of us makes a comment about how fitted sheets are a nuisance. It's a ritual.

I grunted an assent. "Here, take this," I said and handed him a corner. I said that it looked like it might fit.

"I don't think so," Karl said, adding, "He's all you talk about any more." He put his corner of the sheet onto the corner of the mattress. So we'd got it right.

"What do you mean?" I asked, pretty sure I didn't want to know the answer, and I turned to walk out of the room. "I'm getting some water. You want any?"

"Can't you wait until we finish with this?"

"Yeah," I said, "sure." My diversion had worked. I tucked my corner under. Two down, two to go and then the top sheet, blankets and pillows.

"What I mean is that every thing that happens you bring around to him," he said. He walked to the head of the bed and stood there. I was supposed to move up to the head, too, so that we could put the top part of the sheet on. If he put his corner over first then it would leave the hardest part for me.

I walked up to my side, pulling the sheet along in my hand. "Oh?" I said, being as casual as I could.

"Do you have any idea how many times you've mentioned him today? And it's not even noon?" He tucked in his corner.

"Hey!" I said, "Can't you wait for me?" This isn't the way we're supposed to be doing this. I bent down and wrestled with the sheet and mattress until I'd got the corner under just the way it should be.

I went back to the basket and picked up the top sheet. Nothing was clinging to this one. Karl moved back to the foot of the bed. He said, "It's Al said that and Al said this and Al jumped over the candlestick."

The top sheet billowed as we put it on the bed. The trick was to get the same amount on either side of the bed — enough but not too much. "'One good turn in bed gets all the covers,' Al says. Is Al a blanket hog?"

We pulled the sheet over the foot of the mattress far enough so that we could tuck it under. Next the blankets. "You don't have to get sarcastic," I said.

"Thank you. I'm glad sarcasm is not required," he said. He made no move to lift the mattress though I was bent over and gripping it in my hand. He was looking at me intently, and I realized that he was staring down my shirt. "When did you stop wearing a bra?"

"I haven't stopped. I'm just not wearing one now," I said. "Do you want to tuck this in with me?" But now I was standing, and I'd put my hands on my hips.

"What would Al think if he knew you weren't wearing a bra?" he said.

"I'm not going to dignify that with an answer," I said, dignifying it with an answer. I didn't like the direction this line of questioning was taking. "And it's not exactly relevant is it? It's not like he's a real threat," I said.

"Real enough," Karl said. "Isn't he?"

Together we picked up the mattress and slid the sheet under it. Only the blankets and pillows to go. Finally, without talking we slipped the pillows into their cases and plopped them side by side, fluffy and perfect.

We'd made our bed, and now all that was left for me was to lie in it.

The Rosebud Position Paper

LORRIE WAS A VIRGIN when I met her. At least that's what she said. The topic came up when she was writing an essay about a poem by some dead guy named Herrick. Lorrie, the way she put it, "wasn't gathering rosebuds 'til she was good and ready."

And that was fine with me. Well, not fine. Virginity can be dealt with, but I didn't want the responsibility of, um, taking the most precious possession a girl has (that's what the Sisters taught us)—or, to be short about it, popping her cherry.

Of course, if someone else did it…well, it wouldn't be my fault. That's what I told myself, anyway.

Lorrie had her favorite study place, a carrel on the third floor of the library on the far side from the elevators. That's where I did my work-study job. I kept every book in that section in perfect order. I checked The Library of Congress number of each volume and pulled each book forward to the exact edge of its shelf. When I finished, the shelf I'd tidied made the others around it look sloppy. While I was working, I'd look over at Lorrie and smile. She'd smile back and return to her book.

Sometimes she'd look up, stare at something invisible on the ceiling. While she zoned out like that, she had a habit of crossing her legs, letting her shoe dangle, and jiggling her leg. I swear that I tried not to think about her masturbating. The shoe I remember best was a hot number—red high heels. I swear. Red.

She'd catch me looking at her and laugh out loud, then cover her mouth and finally hold an index finger up over her lips as if shushing herself. And she'd stop jiggling her leg.

You could tell where I'd been working because the books were all on their shelves perfect. If some one messed with them, I'd have everything straightened during my next shift. It wasn't easy keeping my work all on that floor. I brought in a lot of doughnuts, the best I could do in the way of bribes.

Even though I was a freshman, I had connections. My roommate's cousin was a ZBT, short for Zeta Beta Tau or Zillions Billions and Trillions. The kid next door was on the football team. My Resident Advisor was a junior Phi Beta Kappa. One of them was bound to be her type. Don't get me wrong, I didn't come straight out and say, "I need someone to fuck her—just once (OK, two, three times tops)."

No, I just mentioned how, where I worked in the library…a phrase here about her hair, another about how her sweater shows a sliver of skin when she stretches, a suggestion about a geometric blue tattoo in the small of her back (or sometimes I said just below her beltline, a butterfly). The tattoo was a lie, but I thought it was incentive. I told the RA flat out that she had a gold navel ring. I didn't exactly say she "did it," but I left out the rosebud position paper.

From my vantage point in the stacks or crouching behind the cart of books, I watched them all court her. I pushed the cart to the best place to listen in. Nobody pays much attention to the guy shelving books. But Lorrie knew I was there. I could tell. Sometimes she left with them and ducked her head down so that her hair fell over her face when she walked by the aisle I was in. I'd watch her toss her head to shake her hair out of her eyes, and once a ZBT actually brushed it off her face himself while they walked. I wanted to deck him.

We'd still talk, though not as much. To tell the truth, I began to feel a bit like a stalker. I didn't hang around her dorm or anything, but I did go to the parties where I knew she'd be. I'd grab a beer and pretend to be having fun while I kept tabs on her.

If she went to one of the bedrooms, I'd find an excuse to go upstairs and hang around the bathroom until she came out, and I'd try to tell if she'd crossed the line. I figured if she was in there for more than an hour—that was it. And I studied the guy's face to see if he looked pissed or pleased.

I needed a project for psychology. I considered doing something on the correlation of duration-of-stay-in-a-bedroom-at-a-fraternity party and class standing. I abandoned the idea when I realized I couldn't get enough data, but I figured I could use it as an excuse if someone asked me what I was doing hanging out up there. No one asked.
My RA did say, "Thanks, kid." At least the bastard ought to know my name.

My plan was that I'd email her during the first week of the next semester. Ask for a date. Something away from the library. I could ask her about her term paper on Herrick. And on, maybe, our fifth date I'd nail her. Guilt free.

I never figured she'd come back to school wearing a ring with the smallest diamond I'd ever seen. Her fiancé's a senior at State. One of us is a lucky man.

Should, Shouldn't

"People who feed songbirds shouldn't keep cats," Franny said as I drove, "especially, feed strays." I heard our mother's tone in her voice, and I was amused because Franny had hated being told what she should and shouldn't do. When we were teenagers she'd sit on her bed in our room and chant, "Should, shouldn't, shit."

"Shh, Franny," I'd say, "She'll hear you, and we'll both get in trouble."

"Are you telling me I should shut up?"

"I'm saying that if you don't shush we'll get both in trouble, that's all."

Somehow we never did. Not for that. We caught it for the usual: undone chores, curfew violations, when the neighbors called the cops because we gave a loud party the one time our mother left us home alone for a weekend. "I guess I can't leave you two alone after all," she'd said, her voice a mixture of anger and frustration. Much later I realized that she was chiding herself as well.

And now Franny was telling me how to live. "Should, shouldn't, shit," I said.

"You know I'm right," Franny said, and then she told me how the cat would leap up on the terra cotta bird bath and break it.

I began chanting Franny's, "Should, shouldn't, shit."

She told me how the cat would get the baby finches in the nest on the lamp next to the front door.

I chanted louder.

She told me about the presents the cat would bring, the tribute of the half-dead mouse or, she said, practically shouting now, the wounded bird.

I chanted louder still.

"Someday you'll see," she said, "You'll see I was right. You'll learn the hard way, and you'll be sorry."

I kept on chanting Franny's teenage chant; in response she kept on scolding, warning me with mounting frustration. I kept on chanting to hear the echo of our mother's voice fill the car. In her lap, Franny held two beautiful stones. It was our first time like this, the two of us alone, going to visit her grave.

Peach Season

THE SUMMER HER PARENTS SENT HER TO LIVE WITH HER FATHER'S BROTHER, Tom and his newest wife, Alice, Jessie was nine. She stayed all summer in their small brick house. Her bed was under the sloping roof. She was happy in their house and on the concrete porch. She liked playing in the yard surrounded by the chain-link fence. A peach tree grew in the front yard, and all summer she watched and waited as the peaches ripened.

She sat on the steps in the sun and felt the heat of the steps on her legs, and she felt the heat seep through her cotton shorts. She liked the sun on her face and arms. She held her legs out to get them tanned. Aunt Alice brought her glasses of real lemonade. In a few weeks the peaches would be ready to pick.

And most days while Uncle Tim was at work, Alice and Jessie danced on the linoleum floor of the kitchen, the jitterbug, the cha cha, the foxtrot. Her aunt taught Jessie the steps, how to move her body, sway to the music, She held Jessie tight and taught her to spin and to dip. She taught her how to follow a lead, how to feel the subtle pressure of a hand on her back telling her how to move. She promised that she would show Jessie how to pick the peaches, but they had to wait until they were ripe.

One morning Jessie was going to take her shower when Alice asked if Jessie knew how to wash "there." She pointed to a place below Jessie's navel. Jessie didn't know what her Aunt meant. "I'll show you," she said. She soaped up a washcloth and handed it to Jessie. "Clean yourself," she said. And she watched. "Not like that," she said.

"Between your legs." She watched as Jessie washed. "No," she said. "To be clean you have to wash between and inside. Do you want me to show you?" Jessie said yes, and her Aunt took the soapy cloth and scrubbed and scrubbed. Later that afternoon they picked ripe peaches. They were warm from the sun, and her aunt showed Jessie how to pick, not to tear them from the tree. The ripe ones come off easily. She offered a sweet ripe peach to Jessie, held it in her palm carefully so she wouldn't bruise it.

Summers now, Jessie eats peaches, and remembers.

Pornography

ALTHOUGH I KNEW WHAT WAS PROPER, I'd buttered the whole slice of toast at once and positioned a large spoonful of raspberry jam on its center. I was considering the possibility of generous sweet smears and whether I'd have enough jam to use on the second slice of toast.

My mother hovered. I waited for her to remind me how I was supposed to eat the toast.

Instead she asked me if I remembered my violin teacher, which I thought was a dumb question. For years she'd delivered me to his living room where I stood for an hour near the upright piano and played what I had learned. From one week to the next it seemed to me I made little progress, and I wondered what he was teaching.

My friends who studied music elsewhere learned something of theory. How to transpose. Keys. I simply was given pieces, and when I'd performed them to his satisfaction, I was given the next. For years I didn't question what happened, or didn't. But by the time I stopped the lessons, I wanted something...else. Some transformation during the hour.

The living room had a smell, something like sawdust and maple syrup.

His wife was always in the room. She sat at the piano as though she were going to be called upon to accompany me. Sometimes she played a phrase on the piano, and I was to play it on the violin. They had a son, who was, as we called it then, slow. Most days he came in and listened. I didn't like that, and I was always glad when he left the room. He never stayed long, but he made me nervous. I didn't mind the daughter, who was older than I. She was pretty, and, as far as I knew,

111

didn't play violin or piano. Or maybe she played both. But most of the time I didn't see her at all.

Did I say we lived in a small town?

I suppose I would have heard about it in time. My parents had probably talked about how to break the news to me. He was dead, she said. His wife and son, too. Gas.

She didn't know what had happened to his daughter.

She said they'd been making movies and got caught. It took a while before I understood what she was talking about. His wife and a man. I suppose he would have lost all his pupils. But he could have moved. Probably the daughter did move. Maybe they thought it would spoil her chances if she'd had to take her brother right then while she was so young.

The way my mother told it, he didn't have a choice. I thought about the films. Black and white. Grainy. It was in the newspaper, my mother said, as though that answered my question about why they had to die.

I spread the jam, red and thick.

The Vorpal Blades

ARMS FULL, MARK STANDS WEDGED WITH THE SCREEN DOOR AT HIS BACK. He shifts the brown bags, propping them up with his knee against the door while he maneuvers. Heddy sits at the kitchen table watching her husband and sets her jaw even before she hears the key turn in the lock.

The kitchen fills with fresh damp air.

"I guess I don't have to ask where you've been," she says, her tone flat, looking at him over the rim of her coffee mug.

"Not if you can read or if you have any common sense. I know you can read," he says. The bags say "Central Hardware" in big red letters.

The April sun falls in tidy squares on the speckled green linoleum and on the Formica table where just moments before Heddy sat listening to the house tick. A mug of coffee sits surrounded by a shoal of plant catalogs.

"Were they crowded?"

"The first sunny weekend? Jammed. You know how it gets. Maybe not. You hardly ever want to go."

"I guess I don't."

"Your friend Martha Ann used to be a hardware junkie. She loved to go in and talk up the hard goods." Mark leans against the counter, the bags on their sides behind him. "She sure liked men."

"I remember," she says. She picks up a catalog and opens it. She does remember. She'd walk into a room and the two of them would be in there laughing, and when they saw her they'd shoot each other a look about as subtle as a supermarket tabloid headline.

"Whatever happened to good old Martha Ann? I don't hear you talk about her much since that week she spent here last summer."

"Were there any good sales on garden things?"

"Yes, she liked men, all right," Mark says as though he's bringing a basket of kittens to a kindergarten.

"Sometimes at this time of year you can get a good buy on peat moss and stuff," she says, then asks, "What was it you said you went for?"

"I didn't say. You were still sleeping when I left."

Heddy hadn't been sleeping. She tries to concentrate on how her hand feels in the sun. "I haven't been sleeping well."

Heddy studies Mark's face, finds nothing, but decides to turn to a safer topic anyway. "Let's see what you got."

"You've been talking in your sleep again. Bad dreams." He doesn't want to let this go.

"You noticed." She can't keep her voice even. She's heard herself screaming in her sleep, felt the terror in her moans.

"You've been keeping me awake," he says.

"Loving as always." He used to wake her when she had nightmares, hold her in his arms until she slept.

"That's me. Devoted."

Heddy walks over to the coffee maker. It's nearly empty, but she says, "Coffee? "

"I stopped at the diner for breakfast."

"Those hash browns and eggs will kill you."

"Don't hold your breath. Not in your life time."

Through the window Heddy sees the bright golden arcs of the forsythia and thinks that they hold all the sunlight of spring in their wild curves.

He peers down at what she's reading. "I see you're back to mooning over catalogs."

"You know I want to put in perennials, ones I can count on every year. Like the forsythia that was here when we came."

"Why can't you be happy with marigolds and petunias? Other women are."

What other women, she wonders, the ones with children? "If we had put in the bulbs when I wanted to, we would've had daffodils and tulips and crocus now for years."

"So? That's your favorite song. If we had done this, if we had done that."

Neither of them says anything for a while. Mark paces, and stands again at the counter. "You're the original Miss If-coulda-shoulda. Heddy-if-coulda-shoulda. Has a ring to it, doesn't it?"

"And I want to plant baby's breath and roses. And chrysanthemums for fall."

In her fantasies she plants and replants, landscaping the yard to perfection. She wants lilacs and hydrangea, big old-fashioned blue hydrangeas, and she wants a peegee hydrangea that would start white and then turn pink and bronze in August. She would make arrangements of the dried flowers.

"How impractical can you get."

She looks out at the bright tangle of forsythia swaying in the wind, graceful as a girl.

It is at this moment that Heddy decides she wants to be buried in the back yard, planted in full sun. She tries out a series of locations. She imagines Mark amiable, cooperative, docile, as he digs one grave after another for her.

She smiles at the thought.

"What's up with you?" he asks.

"What did you buy?" she says.

"Stuff. Lots of stuff. But look at this." He rummages through the bags and pulls out a pair of clipping sheers. "Look." He releases the safety catch and holds them in the air to cut through imaginary branches.

"Vorpal," she says. "Very vorpal."

"What?"

"Snicker snack," she says, pleased to have thought of it. She repeats, "The vorpal blades," not caring that he doesn't understand.

"I can hardly wait to get to that forsythia. I've wanted to do this for years."

"Mark," she says, then stops. This is the first time he's said that he wants to cut the forsythia. She's sure.

"Look, when I get through it'll be a big yellow ball just like the sun. You'll see. Come on. Bring your coffee out and keep me company."

Heddy remembers her vision of an amiable Mark, willing to bury her over and over, no matter how many times she resurfaces. To bury her easily and calmly, wherever she wants.

She stands by his side shivering in the still chilly air. Mark leans into his task, breathless. Through her tears, the blur of golden branches seems like flames. The sheers flash in the sun. The branches fall cold at their feet.

Incident at Finns Point Cemetery

EVEN BEFORE THE MURDER I'd been nervous. It no longer interests me, at least not in the same way it once did. But the fact is that the cemetery is down a long road, and only a small sign notes its presence at the highway. Unless you're making an effort, you might drive right by and have to turn around. Once you're here, there's only that one way out.

The late afternoon sunlight cast the shadow of the obelisk across the perfect lawn. I was returning again to the memorials: the Civil War soldiers, the Confederates marked by the obelisk, the Union dead by a separate monument, covered by a cupola. This ought to be a place of forgiveness, but I suspect the two monuments have been placed so that the shadow of one never falls upon the other.

Off in the corner are graves of German prisoners of war. They have been buried here far longer than they would have been in Deutschland, where graves are reused. Their bones do not belong here, but should be repatriated to their *Heimland*, where their countrymen can make room for them according to their custom, dumping their remains into an unmarked grave by the side of a cemetery in some churchyard. It's what they fought for, *nicht wahr*?

"You believe in ghosts?"

I hadn't been aware of a car driving up. I must have looked alarmed.

"I didn't mean to scare you," the man said in an accent I couldn't quite place. His voice was no louder than the rustle of the reeds or the drying leaves of the tall trees, one of which stood by the parking spots, the other by the apparently vacant caretaker's cottage.

He stood about six feet from me, the sun at his back. I couldn't see his face as I had to look into the sun.

117

"Sure," I said, shrugging. "Why not?"

"Not everybody does," he said. "I get in trouble."

I felt the agitation in his voice. I took a step back.

"You see?" he said. "Proof."

I didn't have to ask what he meant, but I did.

"Like that," he said, with a gesture of shoving someone backwards. He paused, then added, "I got a camera. Pictures."

"What?"

"Something, anyway." He swayed some from left to right and back again. "Hadn't expected anything, but…"

"Sometimes you don't get what you expect."

"And sometimes you do. An image showed up, she showed up, and…"

Who's "she"? I wondered.

"Whatever," he said. "I have dozens of them."

I'm sure it's an illusion, but because reeds grow on embankments surrounding the cemetery, it feels as though the cemetery is in the bottom of a bowl surrounded by the Delaware Bay.

"You have them with you?" I asked.

He tapped his head. "In here," he said, "catalogued."

I wanted to see his face. I thought if I could shift so that his body blocked the sun, stand in his shadow…I moved, but it didn't work. I didn't want to make a big deal of it so I held still. He made me nervous, but I wanted to hear what he said.

"Think of it," he said, "all those photographs right in my head so I can see them whenever I want. They don't get in the way, either."

I didn't understand what he meant. Unless it was the way some memories get in the way so we can't see what's right in front of our eyes, what's happening now, only what happened before and how we feel about that. "Right," I said, knowing my comment didn't make much sense.

"Read the names?" he asked pointing towards the obelisk.

"Yes," I lied.

"And the names on those," he jerked his head towards the two rows of graves of the POW's.

"Why?"

"Curiosity," he answered.

We'd both been ambiguous, and I'd started it. What question had he answered? Why is he asking or why should I read the names?

"Right in here," he said again, pointing to his head. "And here." He laid his open palm on his chest, kept it there like some dramatic pledge-of-allegiance gesture.

I still couldn't see his face, and right then I didn't like it that he could see mine. Something about that gesture gave me the creeps. "Well," I said, "Enjoy what's left of the day. Nice meeting you." I grinned, nodded.

"Every day," he said, and patted his chest, before giving me a jaunty wave. He stood still on the spot as I left.

My car was alone in the little lot. If he'd walked all the way from somewhere down that long road in the unseasonable heat, he must be a real loony, I thought. Good thing I was getting out of there. I hoped my car started.

At my car I opened the door and stood for a moment to let the heat out before I got in. I looked back and saw him standing in front of the two rows of low stones in the far corner. It looked like his hand was over his heart again. Maybe the angle wasn't right from where I stood, but though I could see how the obelisk and the cupola cast their shadows, and the trees, too, his shadow was invisible, had vanished as though it had been swallowed by the sandy Jersey earth.

Advice

LAURA LOOKED AROUND the kitchen: Stove top a filthy mess, dishwasher full of clean dishes waiting to be put away, a pot with a rim of scorched cheese soaking on the counter, dishpan in the sink with a soup pot and dirty soapy water. She emptied the dishwasher, then cleaned the pot in the dishpan just enough for the dishwasher to finish the job.

She reached into the murky water of the dishpan and cut open the tip of her finger. She pulled out a large, new knife. Had he put it in there or had she done so and then forgotten it?

She hoped he'd done it, not knowing any better, for she'd had warnings from her mother not to put sharp knives in dishpans like that. "You'll cut yourself," her mother had said.

If you don't listen to what your mother says, she'd been taught, something bad will happen. And she had always abided by her mother's advice. Well, almost.

She squeezed her finger and watched the fat red drop swell. She sucked her finger, tasting the blood.

Either way her mother had been right.

Nature Lesson

"HOW DID THE TREES GET THOSE SCARS?" Gretta asked. Her eyes darkened with worry. "Are they like people who get hurt?"

"They're all right," I said. "That's how they grow." She'd been pointing at the birches.

"Oh," she said. "OK. If that's how they grow." She ran off, satisfied, her doll tucked under her arm.

Just like people, I thought, hoping she wouldn't have to learn too soon.

A Wedding Toast for Daddy's Little Girl

MELISSA'S PRACTICING, working on phrasing in the first measures of the Moonlight Sonata, a metronome keeping time for her. She's never looked prettier. She brings us such joy!

I write, shaping my words with care: "My hope is that my daughter's dreams will be fulfilled with this man whom she has chosen to be her husband. To him I entrust her.

"I ask you, her bridegroom, to cherish Melissa with precious care. I have every confidence that you will do so, just as I know that she will do all in her power to be a fine wife. She has had as a model her wonderful mother, Sharon, who was like the woman of valor in the Book of Proverbs. Her devotion sustained me through all the years we were granted. God bless her now, and both of you with happiness and long life."

I fold the paper, seal it in an envelope, write, "To be read at Melissa's Wedding."

Melissa stops playing, asks, "What were you writing, Daddy?" She frowns. "What's wrong? Are you going back to the hospital again?"

I consider how to phrase my answer while the dispassionate metronome marks time.

Flinch

FOR HER TWENTY-SECOND BIRTHDAY Celeste's friends gave her a stapler, a Polaroid camera, and a gift certificate to the photo shop at the mall where she could have a picture of herself scanned, enlarged, and printed on glossy paper. They told her that she could put the staples anywhere she wanted.

No one expected that Celeste would board a train to the city, swing her purple patent leather makeup case up onto the shelf over the seat, wave good-bye through the scratched blur of window, and a year later show up as a real centerfold, wearing only white lace stockings and a half-dozen long looping strands of pearls. She'd changed her name to Xeleste, but the magazine said she still pronounced it Celeste.

In her most famous shot Xeleste posed reclining on a red vinyl banquette below a black and silver sombrero, her head tilted back, her bright red mouth open, eager. She held a burrito in her left hand, looking as though she were about to go Linda Lovelace one better.

The photographer reminded Xeleste of Woody Woodpecker, with a shock of red hair and a laugh to match. He called her "celery", "cellotape", "cellar", and "stellar", but never "Xeleste". Still, he had a way about him, leaning towards her, coaxing in the same tone you'd hear in a stable, so that she'd do anything he said and never flinch. She called him Woody, and when she did, he'd wink. She took up with him, as they said back home.

Woody had a thing for food. He'd told Xeleste that in his family "nurture" was synonymous with "feed." The burrito shot was just one of many photos he took of her with food. She licked a chocolate-coated éclair that was oozing custard cream. She held up to her right breast, just grazing her nipple, a giant, red-glazed strawberry still on its stem. Other than the burrito shot, the most complicated set-up involved a day-glow green Popsicle. Woody's assistant, Mel, knelt off-camera and held the Popsicle into the shot. Xeleste, her blonde hair pulled into a ponytail, posed as though she were crawling towards the slightly down-tilted Popsicle, her mouth open. Working with the Popsicle was tricky because it melted and dripped in the lights. In the end they all decided they liked the effect of the clear drop on the end and the little green puddle. Xeleste never got to even lick the Popsicle, but that was all right because she didn't like lime.

Then a gallery not quite in So-Ho showed Woody's photo collage of close-ups of Xeleste's body parts juxtaposed with extreme close-ups of food: a red raspberry; a ripe mission fig cut open lengthwise, its red pulpy flesh glistening; a mussel, mottled, puckered open, sitting on a half-shell. Woody took her to the opening, and fed her tiny yellow cheese cubes on toothpicks, while she held both of their plastic cups, hers filled with white wine, his with red. He introduced her to the gallery owner as Xeleste, his model, his heavenly body.

After a few months, Xeleste began to grow plump. Woody squeezed her arm between his thumb and index finger as though he were taking its measure with a caliper. He did this several times a week. He still took photos of her, but now only at home, usually in the bedroom, always doing something with food, most often exotic tropical fruit.

One evening Xeleste was in a drugstore where they sold children's books and she picked up Hansel and Gretel. When she saw the witch pinching the children's fingers through the bars of the cage, she began to worry, but she told Woody and he laughed, heh heh heh heh heh.

Xeleste noticed the bars on his windows, and worried that they were designed not to keep out would be evil-doers, as Woody called them, but to keep her in. She told Woody about her fears, for she told him everything, willingly, even eagerly as he fed her. She ate no morsel that he did not put in her mouth. And then one day she wondered aloud why she didn't have a key to the deadbolt lock on the door.

Woody silenced her, stuffing her mouth with chocolate kisses. He blindfolded her and dipped a spoon in a mixture he'd made of cyanide and butterscotch sauce, which she licked from the spoon he held. Dip and lick, dip and lick, dip and lick. He popped another kiss into her mouth, and then dipped his finger into sugar. How sweet it was to her. And then the sweetened poison licked, sucked from the spoon. Again and again and again. He waited until she lay still, and he pushed a silk pillow onto her face.

Finally the only sounds in the loft were Woody's ragged breathing, the hum of the refrigerator, and the midnight traffic from four floors down seeping through the locked barred windows. Woody lowered his face to hers. Just as he knew it would, Xeleste's mouth smelled sweet, chocolate, butterscotch and bitter almond. Woody washed his hands, unwrapped the remaining kisses and ate them all one by one. He made a ball of the shiny foil wrappers and dropped it into the trash. He turned on the trash compactor. Wonderful gadget. Celeste lay as he left her on the sofa, her head tilted back, her bright red mouth open, eternally eager.

Rules of Engagement

ANGELO, HE SAYS, "MARIE, YOU ARE SO FULL OF SHIT." He's putting on his jacket ready to walk out, see. And me, naked, my clothes on the floor and wherever.

And I say, "Angelo, you wouldn't know shit if you saw it on your dinner plate."

And he says, "So that's what it was." And he opens the door, but he doesn't leave.

And I get real quiet. I don't want to talk no more. But he's not leaving. He just stands there, with the door wide open. And then the neighbor's new little black dog runs in.

And Angelo, he tries to get the dog out, and I try too, but the dog doesn't know her name yet, so we chase her around the living room until she gets scared and pees on the floor.

And we both stand there, like, who's going to wipe it up. And I go into the kitchen for paper towels, but I don't complain or nothing. I'm just glad she didn't pee on my clothes or on the rug.

Would you believe when I come back Angelo's sitting in his chair with his jacket still on and the dog in his lap licking his face.

So then the doorbell rings, and I run up the stairs. But my clothes, they're all over the living room.

It's the neighbor looking for her dog, and Angelo, I hear him say to her that she should sit down and would she like a drink and all like it's his place already and my bra isn't on the sofa.

I hear the door slam, and I don't know who all left. So I say to myself, whatever, and go downstairs in my wrapper.

126

And Angelo's sitting there in the chair where he was with the dog, and he has his jacket on. It musta' been seventy-five in there. He likes me to keep the heat up, see, and he's wearing his winter jacket. Whatever.

"Your neighbor's a ditz," he says, and he jerks his head over towards the door. And he says like he's surprised, "She took the dog."

And I say, "You thought maybe the dog was gonna be here for a sleepover?" And he doesn't say anything back, but he doesn't move neither. So I say, "You staying or what?" And I'm holding my wrapper closed.

So he says, "You care, if I go or no?"

And I say, "It matters to you, I care? You said I was full of shit."

And Angelo, he says, "You said I wouldn't know shit if you gave it to me for dinner." Which you know I never said, right? He should learn to listen better.

And we go around and around like that, until I think, whatever, let's take it upstairs, and after, he says it's okay we have the caterer my cousin used for her wedding. I told you our colors? Black and silver. They spray the flowers real nice.

ACKNOWLEDGMENTS

"Casseroles," *The Pedestal,* August 2008; "Undertow," *Rumble,* Spring 2007; "Pornography" and "Brood," *Ghoti,* Spring 2007; "Civil Ceremonies," *Literary Mama,* March 1, 2007; "Nature Lesson," *Salome,* October 30, 2006; "Souvenir," *The Pedestal,* August 2006; "Date," *Salome*, March 12, 2006; "Once Removed," *The Green Muse,* May/June 2006; "Girl Waiting," *Underground Voices,* February 2006; "Just One," *Salome,* January 23, 2005; "The Rosebud Position Paper," *Twenty1Lashes,* Issue 1, Winter 2005-2006; "Should, Shouldn't," *Ghoti Magazine*, January 2006; "Even Without Hills," *Midwest Poetry Review*, Fall 2005; "Smoke," *Zink Zine,* Fall 2005; "Journey," *Zink Zine,* Fall 2005; "Ferret Anxiety," *The Beat*, October 10, 2005; "Pesto," *3711 Atlantic,* October 2005; "A Wedding Toast for Daddy's Little Girl," *Antithesis Common*, September 2005; "Cindy's Case," *Salome Magazine*, September 26, 2005; "Two of A Kind," *Defenestration*, September 2005; "Advice," *Skive,* September 2005; "Perfectly Sober," *Girls with Insurance,* August 24, 2005; "Just Desserts," *The Pedestal Magazine,* Augus 2005; "Rules of Engagement," *Thieves Jargon*, August 12, 2005; "Cowboy Poet," *Thieves Jargon*, June 10, 2005; "Score," *Thieves Jargon*, March 4, 2005; "A Virtually True Account...," *Offcourse,* Winter 2005; "Sunshine," *3711 Atlantic,* Winter 2004-2005; "Language," published as "First Date," *The Beat,* Issue 4, December 2004; "Ridiculous," *Pindeldyboz,* November 1, 2004; "Just Another Jack," *Thieves Jargon,* November 4, 2004; "Niagara," *Amsterdam Scriptum*, November 2004; "Pawn," *The Dead Mule,* November 2004; "An Old Story," *Writers Bar,* October 14, 2004; "Easy," *The Shore Magazine,* October 14, 2004; "Peach Season," *The Glut,* November 2004; "Stone," *The Hamilton Stone Review,* Issue 18, Summer 2009; "Hag," *Salome Magazine,* September 13, 2004; "The Vorpal Blades," *Word Riot,* September 2004; "Maintenance," *SmokeLong Quarterly,* Fall 2004; "The Answer," *edificeWRECKED,* August 2004; "Countdown for a Single Girl," *Rumble,* August 2004; "Ramona," *The Staple Quarterly,*

Inaugural Issue, August 2004; "Lucky," *The Beat,* July-August 2004; "Freudian Slip," *Yankee Pot Roast Literary Magazine,* July 2004; "Convictions," *Southern Ocean Review,* Issue 32, July 2004; "Flinch," *The Glut,* July 2004; "Hay," *HiNgE, July* 2004; "The Patsy," *Toasted Cheese,* June 2004; "Drowning," *Slow Trains,* June 2004; "Showtime," *Storied World,* June 2004; "Armor," *Littoral,* March 2004; "Tines," *Salome,* October 26, 2009.

About the Author

MIRIAM N. KOTZIN, associate professor of English at Drexel University, directs the Certificate Program in Writing and Publishing and teaches creative writing and literature. Her fiction and poetry have been published widely in literary journals. She is a contributing editor of *Boulevard* and a founding editor of *Per Contra: the International Journal of the Arts, Literature and Ideas.* She is the author of *A History of Drexel University* (Drexel University, 1983) and two collections of poetry, *Reclaiming the Dead* (New American Press, 2008) and *Weights & Measures* (Star Cloud Press, 2009).

www.ingramcontent.com/pod-product-compliance
Lightning Source LLC
Chambersburg PA
CBHW020626250626
47154CB00004B/1681